Resourceful, he thought. That was Risa.

He felt a familiar tug low in his gut, a pull of attraction and admiration and awe, all wrapped up in one small, brilliant woman. And then, like a slow-rolling detonation, the delayed impact of the reality he'd been tamping down beneath his game face finally hit him with devastating force.

She's alive.

Shock waves of pent-up emotion blew through him, and he ended up dropping to the cold bus stop bench before his knees buckled.

He took several deep breaths, his heart hammering as if he'd run for miles. Risa sat beside him, her compact body warm, and she put her hand on his arm.

"What's wrong?"

How could he tell her what he was feeling when he couldn't trust the emotions? Yes, he was thrilled beyond words that she was alive. He had mourned her deeply, longed for her when she was no longer within his reach, but those feelings seemed to belong to another person.

A person who couldn't have imagined that his wife would let him believe she was dead when she was very much alive.

And carrying his child.

KENTUCKY CONFIDENTIAL

PAULA GRAVES

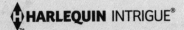

HARLEQUIN INTRIGUE®

For my editor, Allison, whose Raylan Givens love
led to this series.

Recycling programs
for this product may
not exist in your area.

ISBN-13: 978-0-373-69935-3

Kentucky Confidential

Copyright © 2016 by Paula Graves

Printed in U.S.A.

www.Harlequin.com

Paula Graves, an Alabama native, wrote her first book at the age of six. A voracious reader, Paula loves books that pair tantalizing mystery with compelling romance. When she's not reading or writing, she works as a creative director for a Birmingham advertising agency and spends time with her family and friends. Paula invites readers to visit her website, paulagraves.com.

Books by Paula Graves

Harlequin Intrigue

Campbell Cove Academy

Kentucky Confidential

The Gates: Most Wanted

Smoky Mountain Setup
Blue Ridge Ricochet
Stranger in Cold Creek

The Gates

Dead Man's Curve
Crybaby Falls
Boneyard Ridge
Deception Lake
Killshadow Road
Two Souls Hollow

Bitterwood P.D.

Murder in the Smokies
The Smoky Mountain Mist
Smoky Ridge Curse
Blood on Copperhead Trail
The Secret of Cherokee Cove
The Legend of Smuggler's Cave

Visit the Author Profile page at Harlequin.com for more titles.

CAST OF CHARACTERS

Connor McGinnis—His wife, Risa, died in a terrorist attack almost eight months ago. Or did she? A surveillance photo of a pregnant Kaziri immigrant leads the former Marine on a search for the truth. But can he live with what he finds?

Risa McGinnis, aka Yasmin Hamani—She's come to terms with living a lie to protect herself and the child she's carrying. But when the past she left behind storms into her new life, everything she's fought to preserve may be destroyed.

Martin Dalrymple—Risa's only contact with her past has gone silent. Why has he stopped communication with her? Is his own life in danger?

Alexander Quinn, Maddox Heller and Rebecca Cameron—Connor's bosses at Campbell Cove Security Services have promised their support in his search for the truth about his dead wife.

Farid Rahimi—Risa's boss at the restaurant where she works undercover as a waitress named Yasmin pings her danger radar. But why?

Tahir Mahmood—The brutal terrorist was presumed dead after an explosion years ago. But is it possible he's still alive? And could he be behind the ongoing threats to Risa's life?

Jesse Cooper—Convinced someone high in the government may be trying to kill Risa, Connor reaches out to this security expert with experience dealing with government conspiracies.

Leland Garrett—Is the Homeland Security agent friend or foe?

Chapter One

"She's dead," Connor McGinnis whispered, though his eyes declared the words a lie.

On the street below his window, the woman he was surveilling tugged her faded coat more tightly around her swollen belly and waited for the chance to cross the street. A light wind swept snow flurries in small white eddies down the street and threatened to whip the gauzy *roosari* from her head. Grabbing the scarf as it slid down to reveal the dark luster of her wavy hair, she tugged it back into place, but not before he got a look at her face.

Her intimately familiar face.

She looked tired and careworn, but there were no signs that she'd been injured. Of course, the crash had happened months earlier. She might have had time to heal from even a serious injury.

Though how she'd survived the blast in the first place...

He tamped down a maelstrom of conflicting emotions. Not yet. Emotions on the battlefield could be deadly. And if Risa was still alive, he was already engaged in a war he hadn't known about only a few days ago.

If Risa was still alive. He couldn't quite bring himself to believe it yet, no matter what his eyes were telling him. He'd seen news footage of the wreckage found floating in the water off the coast of Japan. Even if someone had survived the bomb blast that sent the jet hurtling into the Pacific Ocean, no one would have come out of that crash unscathed. And Risa's name was on the passenger manifest, which meant she'd gotten on the plane.

He didn't know how this woman could be Risa, no matter how much she looked like her.

Except there were ways to fake passenger manifests, weren't there? Ways to fool transportation security. It was one of the biggest nightmares facing national security agencies worldwide.

Traffic cleared momentarily, and the woman started across the street. Her gaze darted around, right and left, in front and behind, as she made the short transit from one corner to another.

Hypervigilant, he thought.

Reasonable, he supposed, for a refugee from war-torn Kaziristan.

Or for a woman hiding from her past.

Stop. It's not Risa. It can't be.

He was grasping at straws. Letting what he wanted get in the way of what actually was.

That was a good way to drive himself insane. He had to keep his emotions out of the equation. Think logically. Deal in facts.

If Risa had survived the crash, she'd have found a way to let him know.

Wouldn't she?

He lost sight of the woman—the woman who couldn't possibly be Risa—as she turned at the corner and walked under the narrow awnings of the storefronts below the shabby apartment he'd rented earlier that morning. He resisted the urge to run to the ground floor and follow her down the street. It wasn't time to make that particular move.

Not yet.

If ten years of combat had taught Connor McGinnis nothing else, it had shown him the value of patience.

SHE WAS BEING WATCHED.

Inside her apartment, the woman known as Yasmin Hamani locked the door behind her and paused in the entryway to listen. The apartment building was old, prone to settling with creaks and groans of aged wood and plaster, but she didn't sense the presence of another living being within the walls of the small one-bedroom apartment. Still, she unlocked the drawer of the table by the door and withdrew her compact Glock 23, feeling instantly safer.

These days, it was harder to carry a weapon than rely on her disguise to keep her safe. None of her shoulder-carry holsters fit comfortably anymore, thanks to the swell of her pregnant belly. And forget trying to work with any sort of waistband holster.

She made a circuit of the empty apartment with the

Glock in hand before she finally relaxed and put the weapon on the side table where she could easily reach it. She removed the *roosari* covering her hair, relieved to be shed of it for a while. She wasn't Muslim, but the majority of the Kaziri refugees who lived in this section of Over-the-Rhine were, and she donned the head scarf as both protection and concealment.

It was unlikely she'd run across anyone she'd dealt with during her years in Kaziristan, but a dead woman couldn't be too careful. She couldn't afford to stand out.

The baby was fussy this afternoon, turning flips in her womb. Impatient, perhaps, to greet the world outside. Yasmin rubbed her bulging belly, smiling a little at the thumps of the baby's kicks against her palms, strong and reassuring.

The baby was her reason for everything she did these days.

She eased into her desk chair, now used to the dull pain in the small of her back from carrying the tiny burden inside her. She typed in the complex password to her laptop computer and checked her email for any message from her former handler.

Nothing.

She sighed, leaning against the back of the chair. If someone had seen through her cover, apparently Martin Dalrymple didn't know about it.

Which meant what? That she was imagining things?

Working in covert operations had a way of making a person see shadows where none existed. Operatives got used to paranoia. Expecting the worst, seeing threats everywhere you looked, kept you vigilant. And vigilance kept you alive. But she'd thought she was done with that life. She had started a new life, one that wouldn't include dead drops and secret identities. One that included stability and trust. Love.

She should have known better.

The baby kicked again, reminding her that she hadn't lost everything. The pregnancy had come as a shock, a complication her analytical mind had deemed an unacceptable risk.

But her heart had wrapped itself around the tiny life growing inside her like a coat of armor, determined to keep the baby safe from danger.

She would give her baby the life he or she deserved, no matter what it took. Somehow, she'd figure out a way to do it.

But she didn't think it could be here in Cincinnati.

She sent a coded email message to Dalrymple, trying to be as oblique as possible so that even if someone managed to break the cipher, he'd still have to figure out what the hell she was talking about. While Dalrymple knew her well enough to understand what she was trying to tell him, there wasn't anyone else in the world who knew her that well.

Not anymore, anyway.

The baby gave another kick. She was only four weeks away from her due date, though her obstetrician seemed to think she might deliver late. First babies often took their own sweet time.

Rubbing her belly, she logged off and closed the

laptop, hoping Dalrymple would respond soon. The last thing she needed in the final days of her pregnancy was this kind of stress.

Come on, Dal. Tell me I'm imagining things.

She settled in the rocking chair she'd picked up at a thrift store. Most of her furniture was secondhand. Her clothes as well.

She'd never been wealthy, and she could remember plenty of lean times in her life, both as a child and later as an adult. But life as a pregnant Kaziri refugee was proving to be a whole other level of needy. And there was no hope of ever going back to the life she'd once lived.

From down the hall, faint strains of an old Kaziri folk song added a discordant counterpoint to the Bing Crosby tune playing on the radio in the apartment next door. Refugees had taken over several of the empty apartments in the building, but there were a few native Cincinnatians who'd been living in Over-the-Rhine for decades, through bad times and good. Some of them eyed the newcomers with suspicion and even fear, at times signaling their defiance by shows of blatant patriotism in case the refugees forgot where they were living now.

Yasmin felt strangely caught in the middle, someone who knew all the words to both songs clamoring for attention. Her mother had sung "Nazanin" to her as a lullaby for as long as she could remember. And Bing's "White Christmas" had always been one of her father's favorite songs.

It would have been easier if Dal had placed her

in the Raleigh, North Carolina, area, where another group of Kaziri immigrants had started to form their own small cultural enclave. Those Kaziris came from the small Christian community, with its more westernized habits and customs. She could have fit in there quite easily, given her mother's background.

But she wasn't going to find what Dalrymple was seeking in North Carolina. So there would be no Christmas lights this year. No holly wreath on her door or stockings on the mantel. Not if she wanted to fit in with the rest of the Kaziri community here in Cincy.

Still, as she rocked slowly in the chair, making herself wait a little longer before she checked for Dal's return email, she found herself humming along with Bing, feeling a little melancholy.

Christmas was only a couple of weeks away. And this year, she'd be spending it alone.

"Is it her?" Maddox Heller's drawl rumbled through the phone receiver, bracingly familiar.

Connor stepped away from the window. "I'll admit, it looks like her."

"But you're not certain." Heller's voice was tinged with sympathy. A former marine, like Connor, he'd gotten in touch after the plane crash and Risa's death, first to offer his condolences, and later, the new job that had eventually brought Connor to Cincinnati.

"No, I'm not certain." Connor had come to terms with the fact that he wanted to believe the woman he'd seen was Risa. But self-deception during a mission was a great way to end up dead or captured. "The woman is definitely pregnant."

"How far along?"

"How the hell would I know?" He heard a tinge of bitterness in his voice and quelled it. Stick to the facts. "Big. Probably last trimester."

"If it's Risa," Heller said quietly, "then…"

Then the baby could be his. "I know."

"Quinn has feelers out to some of his old contacts at the agency, but if she's part of an ongoing operation, they're not going to tell him anything."

"Do you think…" Connor swallowed and started again. "Do you think she could have planned it all along?"

"What? Faking her death?"

"Yeah."

"I don't know. CIA folks can be a little squirrelly, but…"

But she loved me, he thought. *She loved me, and we didn't have secrets.*

Self-deception, he reminded himself. Always dangerous.

"I think she must live in this area. The Kaziri refugee community seems to be centered here near the new mosque on Dublin Street," he told Heller. The mosque had once been a Methodist church, according to some of the locals he'd talked to earlier that morning. With the exodus of locals and the advent of the refugees, a lot was changing in the neighborhood. Longtime diners had become halal markets and restaurants. A boutique down the street from the mosque now sold hijab coverings for women.

"That's what our intel says," Heller agreed.

By intel, he suspected Heller meant an undercover asset. Maybe more than one. Connor was new to Campbell Cove Security and the academy the company ran. He had a feeling there was a lot about the company he had yet to discover. And other things, he suspected, he might never discover unless there was a pressing need to know.

Heller broke the silence that had fallen between them. "What's your gut on this?"

How the hell was Connor supposed to answer that question? He'd spent the past three days since spotting the pregnant woman in the surveillance photos trying not to feel anything at all, in his gut or anywhere else. If he let himself feel, then he'd lose any chance of dealing with the situation with reason and logic.

"I don't know," he answered. "I can't let my gut lead here."

He wanted to believe way too much to trust his gut about anything where Risa was concerned.

"What are you going to do next?" Heller asked.

Connor checked his watch. Nearly two thirty. "The operative says she works the dinner shift at The Jewel of Tablis, right?"

"Not every night, but yeah."

"So I guess I'll wait a couple of hours and then go have myself a nice halal dinner."

BY THE TIME Yasmin had to leave the apartment to get to her job at the restaurant, she still hadn't heard from Dalrymple. Going on twelve hours since their last contact. Dal had always been the kind of man who lived on his own timetable, but he'd never taken this long to get back to her.

Unless something had gone wrong.

As she tied her apron above the swell of the baby, she glanced around the restaurant, trying to remember the feeling she'd had before while walking home from the doctor's office. A tingle on the back of her neck that said, "Someone is watching."

She supposed it was possible a lot of people were watching her. Pregnant women living alone weren't the norm in a culture like Kaziristan's. She had lived there with her mother for three years while her father was doing a tour of duty overseas. At least, that's what her mother had told her, though she sometimes wondered if the Kaziristan years had come during a rough patch in her parents' marriage.

They'd stayed with her mother's brother and his family, and the experience had been eye-opening, not always in a good way. But during those years, she'd learned a lot about being a Kaziri woman. While a large swath of Kaziristan was cosmopolitan and culturally advanced, some of the rural areas were still deeply tribal, including the part where her mother's brother lived. Those areas were patriarchal in a way people in the West couldn't really comprehend.

But even in those parts of Kaziristan, women had ways of getting things done beneath the veil. It was a lesson she'd never forgotten, and she was banking on that lesson to get her through the next few months of her life.

"Yasmin?" The sharp voice of the restaurant manager, Farid Rahimi, jerked her back to attention. She turned to look at him, trying not to let her dislike show.

He was a short man, and lean, but she knew from observation that he was strong and fast. He was also mean, keeping his employees in line with threats and derision. He was a US citizen, which put him in a far more stable position than most of the people in the community, including all of his employees. Most were here on temporary visas or provisional refugee status, and he made sure they understood just how perilous their lives in the States really were.

"There are a couple of special guests coming tonight. They want the prettiest of the serving girls to wait on them exclusively." He flashed her a bright smile before adding, "So Darya will be serving them. You'll have to pick up her tables."

"Yes, sir," she answered in Kaziri, trying to ignore the flash of cruelty in his smile. One of the hardest things about pretending to be a Kaziri refugee was behaving as if she was resigned to being at the mercy of others.

In another life, she would have cut him in half with her words. And he'd be lucky if she'd stopped there.

"Speak English," Farid added in a harsh tone. He waved one sinewy hand at her head. "And cover yourself."

She reached up and straightened her *roosari*, tugging it up to cover her hair. *It's all part of the assignment*, she reminded herself as she picked up her order pad and went to work, her teeth grinding with frustration.

The conversations she overheard as she worked were unremarkable. Despite its location in the heart of the Kaziri refugee community, The Jewel of Tablis was beginning to draw patrons from all over Cincinnati. In fact, most of the refugees Yasmin knew were too impoverished to eat out, though most of them shopped in the small halal food market attached to the restaurant. So far tonight, all of her diners were English-speaking Americans. Not one of them said anything that might have piqued Dalrymple's interest.

She was beginning to wonder why he'd wanted her to move here to Cincinnati rather than simply relocating her somewhere out West, where she could live in solitude and see trouble coming for miles before it arrived.

"Darya!" Farid's voice rose over the ambient noise of conversing diners, drawing Yasmin's gaze toward the door where he stood. There were two dark-featured men, each wearing an expensive *payraan tumbaan*, the traditional long shirt and pants typical in Afghanistan, Pakistan and, these days, the Kaziri moneyed class. The intricately embroidered silk vests the two men wore over their shirts were definitely products of Kaziristan, adorned as they were with the brilliant-hued fire hawk of Kaziri folklore.

She didn't recognize either man, though the taller man on the right looked oddly familiar, even though she was certain they'd never met. Maybe she'd run across one of his relatives during her time on assignment in Tablis, the Kaziri capital city.

She'd kept a low profile while she was there, playing a similar role blending in with the native Kaziris in order to keep an ear close to the ground during a volatile time in the country's downward spiral toward another civil war. Strange—and alarming—that she'd been afforded more autonomy and respect as a woman in Kaziristan than she was as a woman in the insular Kaziri community in Cincinnati.

On the upside, being pregnant and makeup-free was working in her favor here. People saw the round belly first and never bothered letting their gazes rise to her face, especially with more nubile, exotic-looking beauties like Darya and her bevy of young, unmarried friends to draw the attention of Kaziri men. And the Americans as well, she noted with secret amusement, as the middle-aged male patrons she was currently serving kept slanting intrigued glances at Darya as she walked with sinuous femininity to the VIP table to take their orders.

Out of the corner of her eye, she noticed another customer enter the restaurant and take a seat at a table near the window. She delivered her most recent order to the kitchen and returned to the dining hall, grabbing a menu and pouring a glass of water before heading to the newcomer's table.

A burst of laughter from the VIP table drew her attention in that direction. One of the men was flirting outrageously with Darya, who was eating up the attention with the confidence of a woman who knew her appeal.

Swallowing a sigh, Yasmin turned her attention back to her new customer. He lifted his head, pinning her with his blue-eyed gaze.

Her stomach gave a lurch.

The glass slipped from her hand, but the man whipped his hand out and caught it on the way down. Only a few drops of water splashed across the dark hair on the back of his hand.

He set the glass on the table, still looking at her.

"Hello, Risa," Connor McGinnis said.

Chapter Two

Connor focused his gaze on Risa's pale face, trying to read the snippets of emotion that flashed like lightning across her expression. Within a couple of seconds, her pretty features became a mask that hid everything from him.

"Yasmin," she said quietly as she mopped up the spilled drops of water from the table using a rag she pulled from her apron pocket. Her voice, almost as familiar as his own, came out in a heavy, convincing Kaziri accent. "My name is Yasmin and I will be your server tonight. Would you like to try the mint tea?"

So it wasn't amnesia. There had been a part of him that almost prayed it had been memory loss from the plane crash that had kept her away for so long, but those hopes had been dashed the second her eyes met his. They'd widened, the pupils dilating with shock, before she'd lowered her gaze and set about hiding everything she'd briefly revealed.

He knew what that Kaziri accent hid—a South Georgia drawl as warm and slow as a night in Savannah, where Risa had been born and her parents still lived.

They'd mourned her, too, he thought.

How could she have chosen to disappear the way she had, letting everyone who knew and loved her think she was dead?

He struggled to keep the anger burning in his gut in check, careful not to let it show in his expression. He, too, was good at wearing masks.

"When does your shift end?" he asked quietly.

She pretended not to hear the question. "The special tonight is lamb kebabs with rice."

"We have to talk, Yasmin." He put extra emphasis on her alias.

"No." Her hazel eyes lifted to meet his gaze before she added, "Sir."

"You don't think I have a right to ask a few questions?"

For a second, her mask faltered, fierce emotion burning in her eyes. But she looked away quickly. "Take your time to study the menu. I will return in a few minutes. Would you like something to drink while you are waiting?"

"Mint tea," he said finally.

She gave a nod and walked away. Her gait was subtly different, her back arched from the weight of her pregnant belly. He realized with some surprise that he'd never before imagined what she'd look like pregnant.

How could that be? Why had they never thought about children, about a family?

A few tables away, a slender young woman in a simple, shape-hugging dress and a matching peacock-blue *roosari* was taking orders from two middle-aged men. The one nearest was dressed in an elaborately embroidered *payraan tumbaan*. Connor couldn't get a good look at his face. His companion, however, sat facing Connor, though his gaze was lifted upward to smile at the pretty server. Connor didn't recognize him.

But there was something about the shape of the other man's head, the slight wave of his silver-flecked black hair, that tugged at Connor's memory.

How did he know the man? Was it from those years he'd spent in Kaziristan? Or was the acquaintance more recent?

He sensed more than saw Risa's approach and turned his gaze toward her, watching her walk to his table. She carried a small tray with a glass of iced mint tea, even though he hadn't indicated whether he wanted it hot or cold. She placed the glass of tea on the table in front of him and started to turn away.

"I didn't ask for my tea to be iced," he murmured. But of course, she'd given him ice because she knew that's how he liked it.

She froze in place for a second before she turned and lowered her gaze. "I am sorry. I will bring you another cup."

He closed his hand over hers as she reached for the glass. "Washington Park. Are you familiar with it?"

For a moment, her fingers flexed beneath his grip. But she gave a tiny nod.

He dropped his hand away before they drew unwanted attention. "I will be on a bench near the bandstand by the water park. Tomorrow morning at ten. If you want to talk." He handed her the menu. "Tea will be all. Thank you."

She lifted her gaze to meet his. "The table will be needed once the dinner crowd picks up."

"Understood." He took a couple of drinks of the cold mint tea and realized she'd added a packet of sweetener, the way he liked it. "Thank you for the tea. It's perfect."

She averted her gaze but didn't move right away. He thought he saw a hint of moisture glimmering in her eyes before she finally walked back to the kitchen area.

He released his pent-up breath and glanced at the table nearby where the two Kaziri men continued flirting with the young waitress. It was at that exact moment that the second man turned his head, giving Connor a good look at his profile.

A ripple of unease darted through him. He didn't recognize the man, but something was ringing alarm bells in his head. He felt as if he should recognize him somehow. But why?

He looked at the phone lying on the table in front of him. Unhurriedly, he picked it up and swiped the screen to unlock it. Glancing toward the other table, he pushed the camera application button, bringing up the viewing screen, and slowly angled it toward the men at the other table.

Pretending to send a text, he snapped a quick shot

of the man facing him. He waited for the other man to turn again, but he was looking up at the flirtatious waitress, who seemed to be regaling them with a story in rapid-fire Kaziri.

The clatter of silverware nearby drew his attention away for a moment, until he spotted the toddler at a table near the door who had thrown his spoon on the floor. As the mother shot a look of apology toward the approaching server, Connor looked back at the table where the two Kaziri men sat. The second man had turned in his chair to watch the young mother and child, his expression harsh with disapproval.

He was perfectly framed in the phone's viewer screen.

Connor snapped a couple of photos before the man turned his back again. While he was at it, he took a few other shots, one of the dark-haired man who seemed to be the restaurant manager, another of the pretty young waitress attending to the table where the Kaziri men sat, and finally, carefully, a shot of Risa as she served a nearby table, her *roosari* sliding backward to reveal her dusky hair and delicate profile.

After one more shot, he pocketed his phone and retrieved his wallet. He put a twenty on the table next to the half-empty tea glass before he walked out the door, careful to keep his face averted from the two Kaziri men.

Outside the restaurant, the night had turned bitterly cold, the last fluttering of snow drifting silently from the winter sky. Tugging up his collar to guard his neck from the icy wind, he hurried down the block to a coffee shop angled across the street from The Jewel of Tablis.

A blast of heat welcomed him as he entered. A freckled waitress with straw-blond hair and bright red lipstick greeted him from the counter. "Take a seat, sir. I'll be with you in just a sec."

Connor sat at one of the tables by the window, not entirely happy with the view through the plate glass. The bright interior of the diner reflected back at him, making it difficult to see much of the street outside, though the colorful lights of The Jewel of Tablis were just visible through the reflection.

He pulled out his phone and opened the photo gallery, studying the images he'd snapped at the other restaurant. He'd gotten a good shot of the younger man who had sat facing Connor's table. He texted Maddox Heller a quick message and attached the photo. Then he picked out the best shot he had of the older man and sent the image to Heller as well. Does this man look familiar?

As the waitress arrived with a pot of coffee and a menu, his phone hummed. He took the menu and checked his messages. There was a text from Heller.

Not sure, Heller had written. The image isn't clear. Can you track? Get a better shot?

Will try, he texted back and set his phone on the table in front of him, peering through his reflection at the door of the restaurant down the street.

PANIC BURNED IN her chest, stealing her breath. She forced herself to slow her breathing, to concentrate on staying calm. Thanks to the pregnancy, her blood pressure was a little higher than normal, so she had to deal with the stress for the baby's sake as well as her own.

Don't think about Connor. Don't think about anything but the job.

"Are you okay?" Darya's voice startled her, setting her nerves rattling. Darya had been born in Cincinnati and spoke Kaziri with an American accent.

"I'm feeling a little tired," Yasmin answered, her own Kaziri as authentic as a native's, thanks to her mother and those years spent in Kaziristan, first with her mother's brother and his family, and then undercover with the agency.

Her gaze drifted toward the VIP table. Maybe that's why she'd thought one of those men looked familiar? Had she seen him before in Kaziristan?

Darya followed her gaze and lowered her voice to a soft hiss. "Pigs," she said with a viciousness that caught Yasmin by surprise.

The younger woman's parents put great stock in tradition and they had raised their daughter to observe their customs, but perhaps Darya had a rebellious side. Despite her flirtations with the VIPs earlier, Yasmin now noticed a pinched look around the girl's eyes and mouth that suggested she had found her role vexing.

Not worth the tips they would leave when they departed?

"I think that handsome customer you served earlier liked you," Darya added, her voice back to its normal, teasing tone. "The one with the leather jacket? Very manly."

"I am pregnant and hardly looking my best," she countered, trying to forget the look of betrayal in Connor's eyes. A pain began to throb behind her forehead. "You were right. I am not feeling well."

She had to get out of here. Go somewhere to think. Figure out what to do next. Try to reach Dal again.

"Go. Your shift is nearly over. I will tell Farid you became ill and left."

Yasmin glanced at her watch. It was eight forty-five. The restaurant closed at nine. "I'll tell him," she said, already heading toward the kitchen. Farid would probably dock her the final hour of her pay, but money was the least of her problems at the moment.

How had Connor located her? What kind of game was he playing?

She found Farid in his cluttered office behind the kitchen and told him she was feeling unwell.

"You'll get an hour less in your paycheck this week," he warned her. "Unless you can pick up an hour later this week."

"I will do that," she said, not at all certain she'd be back to the restaurant at all.

Instead of going out the back door into the darkened alley behind the restaurant, she chose the relative safety of the well-lit front exit. As she left, she spared another glance at the two men sitting at the VIP table. They leaned toward each other over the table, deep in conversation. The older man's demeanor seemed angry, while the younger man looked tense and worried. From her vantage point, she couldn't see the older man's face, but there was something vaguely familiar about the way he held himself erect, about the shape of his head and his slim but masculine build.

Flicking her gaze toward the front exit, she realized she could see the older man's reflection quite clearly in the window. Clearly enough that she was now certain she'd seen him before. But not in person.

Where had she seen him?

It might have been on Dalrymple's office wall, she realized a few moments later. There had been several surveillance shots tacked up on a corkboard behind Dal's desk in his Washington office. She'd asked about the photos once, but Dal had brushed her questions aside. "They're wins," he'd said with grim satisfaction. She'd assumed that Dal meant they were bad actors who'd been killed or captured by the agency.

One of the photos on the wall had looked a little bit like one of the two men Darya had been serving earlier, hadn't it?

But those men on Dal's wall of wins were dead or locked up somewhere they'd never escape.

So how could one of them be sitting at table six in The Jewel of Tablis?

And was it a coincidence that Connor had shown up at this restaurant at the same time as the mystery man? Maybe he hadn't come to Cincinnati looking for her at all.

Maybe he was here looking for the mystery man.

She exited the warmth of the restaurant, the shock of frigid air sucking the breath from her lungs. Pulling her coat more tightly around her, she started walking down the street toward the bus stop on the corner. The restaurant was close enough to her apartment to walk there most days, but she was cold, tired and feeling hunted. She could splurge on the bus fare after the evening she'd just had.

Light from the storefronts across the street illuminated her way between the circles of light sporadically shed by streetlamps. On a Wednesday night, the crowd of pedestrians was lighter than it would be on the weekends, but there were enough people to make her feel safer as she walked to the corner. A few of them gave her curious glances, their gazes directed either at her head scarf or her swollen belly. A couple of the women flashed her sympathetic smiles. One of the people sitting on the bus stop bench rose to let her take his place.

She took the seat gratefully and sat to wait for the bus, letting her gaze take in the people walking past. Finally, the bus appeared amid the light traffic moving toward the corner, and she reached into her purse to make sure she had exact change. As she gathered the coins in her hand, she heard a deep voice speaking Kaziri.

"The serving girl was beautiful, no?"

Looking up, Yasmin spotted the two VIPs from the restaurant, walking together alone. She looked away as they neared her, covering her surprise so that no one around her would notice and remember. Then, as the men passed by, the bus arrived, and the people waiting with her at the bus stop moved at once to board.

Yasmin remained where she was until everyone else had started toward the bus. She rose, too, but turned to follow the men instead.

She was far enough away that they weren't likely to hear her footsteps following them. They were certainly showing no signs of stealth themselves, the older of them walking with a confident swagger, his colorful *payraan tumbaan* rippling in the cold breeze with each step.

The men walked two more blocks before turning onto a cross street. The lights here were fewer and spaced farther apart. While she'd been on the main drag, she had been accompanied by a scattering of fellow pedestrians, but once she took the turn to follow the Kaziri men, she was alone, and her sense of vulnerability increased.

In her prime, the prospect of following a couple of men down a dark side street wouldn't have given her much pause. But in her prime, she had never been over eight months pregnant and unarmed.

She slowed her gait, let them move a little farther ahead of her but still close enough that she wasn't likely to lose them unless they tried to shake her tail. Her clothing was dark, and her olive skin and dark hair wouldn't be easily visible as long as she stayed in the shadows.

Cincinnati was still a relatively new place to her, but she'd taken care to study the street maps and familiarize herself with the area for just such a situation as this. When she'd come to town seven months ago, shortly after her previous life had all but ended, she hadn't known she was pregnant. She had intended to be much more useful to Dal than she'd turned out to be.

But the job was still the job, and one of the two Kaziri men she'd spotted at The Jewel of Tablis had pinged her radar, big-time. Maybe she was wrong about seeing him before. Maybe his reason for being in Cincinnati was completely innocent.

Or maybe they were planning to bring al Adar terror attacks to the United States, hiding themselves among the poor immigrants who'd fled Kaziristan to escape unrest and persecution back home.

Near the next cross street, the two men slowed their pace as they reached the side door of a four-story brick building. It was hard to tell much about the place until the door opened, spilling light into the darkened street and revealing a quick glimpse of the dingy redbrick facade. Then the door closed, plunging the street into darkness again.

Yasmin peered at the darkened streetlamp overhead. Was it dark from normal wear and tear, or had someone deliberately disabled the bulb? And if so, was it to hide what was inside the building the two men had entered?

The longer she stayed here in the open, the more danger she put herself in, she realized. She'd wandered away from the safety of foot traffic on the main thoroughfare, leaving her vulnerable. And maybe if she had only herself to worry about, it would have been a risk worth taking.

But the gentle kicks of the baby in her womb reminded her that she wasn't the only person in danger if she lingered here much longer.

She reversed course, walking as briskly as a heavily pregnant woman could, keeping her eye on the bright strip of lights just two blocks ahead. Not much farther to go now.

"You!" a deep, accented voice called out from behind her.

She couldn't keep herself from taking a look.

The door at the end of the block was open, and three men stood in the doorway, staring toward her.

She turned around and started to run.

THE SOUND OF a man's voice calling out, followed by the thud of running footfalls, drew Connor's attention as he paused in the middle of the narrow alley he'd used as a shortcut in hopes of catching up to his quarry.

The footsteps seemed to be coming closer, spurring him into a sprint, his rubber-soled boots quiet on the uneven concrete breezeway. As he neared the opening into the street, he heard the sound of hard breathing. A woman's breathing, he thought. The sound was harsh with fear and desperation.

It was her. He could feel it like a shiver in his bones.

His body reacted on pure instinct, his arms reaching out to catch her as she ran past the narrow opening of the alley. He pulled her into the dark recess, closing his arms around her as she flailed to escape.

"It's me," he whispered in her ear.

She stopped struggling, but he could feel the pounding of her heart where her slender back pressed against his chest. Underneath one arm, something in her abdomen fluttered against his wrist, then thumped solidly against his grasp, making him swallow a gasp of surprise.

He urged her toward the other end of the alley and out of the line of sight. Around the corner of the building was a large trash receptacle. The smells from inside were ripely unpleasant, but it offered a decent hiding place until he could be certain the men who'd apparently been chasing her down the sidewalk had given up.

She huddled close to him, as if seeking his warmth, though she was furnace-hot against his chest. When she spoke, it was barely a whisper. "What are you doing here?"

"Saving you," he answered.

Chapter Three

Her name was not Yasmin Hamani, though every piece of identification she possessed proclaimed her to be so. She was not a widowed immigrant from Kaziristan, though over the past few months she had almost convinced herself she was.

But burrowed into the solid strength of Connor McGinnis's arms, breathing in his familiar scent, hearing the steadying beat of his heart beneath her ear, she allowed herself the truth.

She was Parisa DeVille McGinnis, Risa for short. Her mother was a Kaziri woman who'd married the strapping young US marine who'd saved her from death in a terrorist attack in her war-torn homeland. Risa herself had married a marine, a smart, brave and loyal man she'd met in the mountains of Kaziristan many years later. Like her parents, they'd been on track for their own happily-ever-after.

Until Risa McGinnis had died in a bomb attack on a commercial flight from Kaziristan to the US almost seven months ago. The plane had disappeared from radar over the Pacific and only a few pieces of debris had been found floating in the ocean near the plane's last coordinates on the radar.

All souls lost.

Well, all the souls who'd actually made it aboard the plane.

"We need to get moving." Connor's voice rumbled in her ear. "Lose the *roosari*."

She tugged the scarf from her head and shoved it into the pocket of her coat. She allowed herself a quick look at him, though the sight of his face, so close, so achingly familiar, left her feeling breathless and light-headed.

"How far away do you live?" he asked quietly.

"You can't go there. I live alone, unprotected." The words came out so easily, as if she truly was the woman whose life she'd lived for months now.

"I'm your husband, Risa."

Something inside her chest melted and began to warm her from the inside out. "But they think I'm a widow."

"I hope I died a heroic death." His dry tone should have made her laugh, but her heart ached too much.

"Where are you staying?" she asked. "We could go there."

"It's not far from here." He draped his arm around her shoulder and pulled her closer. "Remember, you're not Yasmin now. You're Parisa. Sexy and smart. You take no prisoners. And you're with me."

She looked at him, her heart breaking. "I'm sorry."

"We'll worry about apologies later." He nodded toward the trash-strewn alley stretching out in front of them. "Ready?"

Risa nodded, ignored the ache in her back and legs, and wrapped her arm around his waist.

Huddled together against the cold, they hurried down the darkened alley until they reached the main drag, where streetlamps lent a twilight glow to the nightlife tableau. It was past ten now, but even on a weeknight, the traffic flow, both vehicular and pedestrian, would continue past midnight.

By the time Connor led her to a shabby-looking walk-up just a couple of blocks east of Vine Street, Risa's back was starting to cramp. To her relief, there was just one flight of stairs to climb before he stopped and led her down the hall to a door marked 201. He unlocked the door and let her inside.

Compared to his place, hers looked almost homey. His living room consisted of a couple of mismatched wooden chairs around a table, and a third chair sat facing the window. A laptop computer lay closed on the table next to a take-out box.

"Have you eaten?" he asked, tossing his keys on the table.

She eyed him warily. His calm, businesslike demeanor wasn't what she'd expected from her husband upon learning she hadn't actually died.

She'd spent the past seven months letting him believe she was dead. If the situation had been reversed, she'd have been furious.

Except he didn't seem furious, either. He seemed… distant.

"Food?" he asked again. "I don't have much here, but I can run across the road to the all-night diner."

"I'm not hungry." She shrugged off her coat and looked around the bare apartment. "But I could use a bathroom."

His gaze dropped to her round belly. "Right." He nodded toward the narrow hallway just off the main room. "It's the door on the right."

The door on the left was open, revealing a darkened bedroom. In the low ambient light seeping into the hallway from the living room, she saw that his bed was little more than a bunk, wide enough to accommodate—barely—a man Connor's size.

This was a mission, she realized as she closed the bathroom door behind her. Not a man looking for his missing wife, but a soldier on assignment. That was why he was so distant.

He was looking at her as his job, not his wife.

Shaking from a combination of cold and delayed reaction, she stared into the wide hazel eyes of the pregnant woman in the cabinet mirror and realized she'd never felt so alone in her life.

No emotions. Emotions are messy and unreliable.

Connor gazed out the window at the street below. The snow had started again, coming down in light flurries. He was glad they were out of the cold for the night.

"Am I staying?"

Risa's soft alto sent a shiver rippling down his spine. He turned to find her standing in the doorway, one shoulder leaning against the frame. The docile young Kaziri widow was gone, and the clear-eyed

CIA agent he'd fallen for three years ago had taken her place.

"I don't think you should risk going back to your apartment."

"I don't have a change of clothes."

"I have a shirt you can borrow." He regretted the words even as they slipped between his lips, for they reminded him of long, sweet nights of lovemaking, followed by lazy mornings with Risa wandering around their apartment in his shirt and little else.

She ran her hand over the large bulge of her stomach. "Make it a big shirt."

He wasn't going to ask. He wasn't. If she had something to tell him about the baby, she would.

Wouldn't she?

The Risa he'd known would have played it straight with him. Always.

But the Risa he'd known wouldn't have let him believe she was dead when she wasn't.

"You must have so many questions," she murmured, walking slowly toward him. She was trying to play it cool and sophisticated, the sexy spy in control, but carrying around a baby inside her was apparently hell on the femme fatale act. She still looked sexy, but in an earth-mother sort of way, all fecund beauty and softness.

He couldn't hold back a smile. "You can drop the act, Risa. You just can't sell it with that beach ball you're carrying under that dress."

She stopped, looking uneasy. "Why aren't you asking the obvious questions?"

He played dumb. "What are the obvious questions?"

"How did you survive the plane crash, Risa?"

"How *did* you survive the plane crash, Risa?"

"I never got on the plane." She took another step.

"Why didn't you call me, Risa?"

He stayed quiet that time, struggling to control a potent storm of anger and hurt churning in his chest.

"Dalrymple pulled me off the flight. He told me there was a price on my head and I needed to lie low. Then we heard the plane crashed."

He looked at her through narrowed eyes, wondering if he could trust what she was saying. It was so pat. So obvious. Hell, maybe she even believed the story herself. Maybe Martin Dalrymple really had pulled her off the plane and told her about a price on her head. The plane crash immediately after his warning was a convincing touch.

A little too convincing, maybe.

"You think I haven't wondered the same thing?" she asked softly, moving another step closer. If he reached out now, he could touch her. Pull her close to him the way he had out in the cold alley. Feel her heart beating against his chest once more, something he'd thought he would never experience again. "You think I didn't wonder if Dal was pulling a scam on me?"

But he kept his hands by his side. "Dalrymple isn't known for his truthfulness."

"I know." She put her hand on her belly. "But if he wasn't lying—I couldn't take the chance. There was too much at stake. Not just me."

His gaze fell to where her hand cupped her round

belly, despite his determination to remain unaffected. "You mean the baby?"

"I didn't know I was pregnant when I agreed to play dead." Her voice was soft, her tone sincere. "I found out almost a month later. But you'd already held the memorial service. You'd left the Marine Corps."

"So, what? You decided that what I didn't know wouldn't hurt me?"

"No, of course not—"

"Because it did." His grasp on his emotions broke, and a flood of anger and old grief poured into his throat, threatening to choke him. "It hurt like all hell. It still does. Every damn day."

Her face crumpled. "I'm sorry."

"Sorry you let me believe you were dead?" He closed the distance between them in one furious step. "Or sorry that I found out you weren't?"

She put her hand on his chest. His brain told him to shake off the touch, but the feel of her palm warm against his sternum, so damn familiar and longed for, nearly unmoored him.

He closed his hand over hers, holding it against his chest. "Do you have any idea what it was like, hearing you'd died on that plane?"

"I'm sorry." Tears spilled down her cheeks, unchecked. "I wanted to let you know, but Dal said you were in danger—"

"Dal said." He spat the man's name with contempt, his anger finding an easier target. "I don't give a damn what Dal said. *You* told me you were quitting,

Risa. We agreed. We were done. It's why you were on your way home from Kaziristan in the first place."

"I know, but—"

"We had a life planned, Risa! You and me and a house of our own in a place we both loved instead of living out of suitcases and passing in the airport, remember?"

She wiped her eyes with her knuckles. "I remember."

He raked his fingers through his hair, trying not to let his emotions get the best of him. *Focus, Marine.* "Who were the men you were following?"

"I don't know," she answered. She sounded as if she was telling the truth, but he realized he just couldn't be certain. Not anymore.

"So why were you following them?" he asked.

She moved toward the window, standing just a little short of it, as if she worried she might be seen from the street. "I shouldn't have come here. People will notice if I don't go home. In some ways, living in an immigrant community can be like living in a small town. Everybody keeps an eye out for everybody else."

He noticed that she had formed a habit of rubbing her belly when she spoke, as if she was soothing the child inside. He didn't want to ask the next question, but he had to.

"Am I the father, Risa?"

RISA HAD BEEN expecting the question. Dreading it, because of what it would mean. But she hadn't realized how much his show of distrust would hurt, even as she understood why he harbored it.

"You're the father," she said simply, because anything else would only exacerbate his doubts.

"And you weren't ever going to tell me I had a child?"

"Honestly, Connor, I hadn't thought that far ahead." She turned back to the window. "I was supposed to be on the plane. But Dal had heard chatter that al Adar had put a target on my back. We knew they had people placed in the airports and other means of transportation."

"So he took you off the plane and sent two hundred and twelve other people to their deaths to fake yours?"

"God, no!" She turned to look at him. "I would never have allowed that. You know that."

"But it's what happened, isn't it?"

He looked so angry, she thought, her own chest tightening in response. Was anger the only feeling he had left for her now?

"He seemed genuinely shocked by the bomb on the plane. Connor, he sent another agent on that plane to take my place so al Adar would think I was going to be landing in San Diego as we planned."

Pain flashed across his expression. "I was waiting there. For hours. They didn't tell us right away that something had gone wrong. I got a call from Jason Ridgeway. He'd seen it on the news. A Russian airliner had disappeared somewhere over the Pacific."

"I'm sorry. It wasn't supposed to happen that way."

He took a deep breath and let it out slowly, raking

his hand through his already-tousled hair. "Okay. You didn't expect the crash. But what about after that? You couldn't let me know you were alive?"

"Dal said—"

"I don't care what Dal said!" His voice came out in a pained roar. He turned his back to her, visibly trying to regain control. She waited silently, giving him time and space to do so.

Finally, he faced her. "I'm sorry. What did Dal say?"

"It doesn't matter. I should have contacted you. I was just—it was one thing to think I was being targeted. But to know that they'd kill over two hundred people just to kill me—"

"Pretty shattering, huh?" For the first time, Connor sounded sympathetic.

"Very shattering." She pressed her palm against the curve of her belly, taking comfort in the gentle wriggling of the baby inside her. He—or she—could probably sense her tension. Not for the first time, she wondered whether she was carrying a girl or a boy. Her ob-gyn had offered her the chance to find out the baby's sex, but she'd wanted to wait until birth.

Until this moment, she hadn't known why she'd wanted to wait. But watching Connor's gaze follow the movement of her hand, she realized she had always hoped that somehow, against all odds, she'd be able to share the birth of this child with her husband.

He might never forgive her for letting him believe she was dead so long, but she had no doubt whatsoever that he'd love their child.

"Why are you here in Cincinnati, pretending to be a Kaziri widow?"

She sighed. "Sometimes, I wonder that myself."

Connor looked at her through narrowed eyes. "You look tired."

"I had to walk eight blocks for my doctor's appointment this morning, and then I was on my feet for hours at work."

"And then you followed a couple of men down a dark street."

"Yeah. Not my finest moment."

He pulled a chair away from the table. "Take a load off."

She took a seat, swallowing a sigh of pure relief. She looked down at her feet and saw that her ankles were looking a little puffy. "Ugh, whoever said women glow when they're pregnant was probably blind or demented. I've just inflated."

Connor smiled, giving her the first glimpse of his dimples in forever. Her heart turned a couple of flips in her chest at the sight, just as it had the first time he'd smiled at her. "You look beautiful. You always do."

The kindness in his voice, the sincerity of the sentiment, drew hot tears to her eyes. "I shouldn't be glad you're here, because you've probably put yourself in terrible danger. But I am. I'm so, so glad you're here."

He started to reach out his hand toward her, but he stopped midmovement and let his hand drop to his lap. "Are you?"

She swallowed her disappointment. "Yes, of course. But how did you find me?"

He reached down and pulled a battered-looking briefcase up to the table, unfastened the buckle and pulled a tablet computer from inside. He swiped his finger across the screen, then tapped a couple of times before he handed the tablet to her.

She looked down and saw a photo of a Free Kaziristan rally that several people in the community had held a couple of weeks earlier. She hadn't attended the rally herself, not wanting to put herself in the spotlight of refugee politics in any way, but the rally had taken place on the street in front of the restaurant. She'd had to pass through the throngs to get to work.

She looked lifeless in the photo. Was that how she always looked?

"I kept telling myself it couldn't be you." Connor's voice rumbled low and soft, like thunder in the distance. "You wouldn't have let me think you were dead. But there you were."

"Connor—"

A loud trio of raps on the door cut her short, the sound sending a hard jolt of alarm down her spine.

"Go to the bedroom," Connor said softly, already on his feet. He pulled a large Ruger pistol from his bag and tucked it in his waistband behind his back, letting his jacket drop to cover it.

Risa hurried down the hallway into the bedroom, her heart fluttering with fear. If someone from the community had seen her come into this apartment with Connor, everything she'd spent the past few months trying to set up would be destroyed.

And she and Connor would be in the worst danger of their lives.

CONNOR LOOKED THROUGH the security lens and saw a familiar face staring back at him. He turned the dead bolt and disengaged the security chain, then opened the door to a bearded man wearing a high-collared shirt and plain khaki pants. His visitor's hazel gaze swept the room quickly.

"Where is she?" he asked.

"Nice seeing you, too, Quinn."

Alexander Quinn didn't wait for an invitation, entering and nodding for Connor to close the door behind him. As Connor reengaged the locks, Quinn crossed to both of the street-facing windows and shut the blinds.

"Heller says it's her. So I tried her apartment. She wasn't home. Then I tried her workplace, and she wasn't there, either."

"I told you I'd handle things my own way." Connor heard the tight annoyance in his own voice but couldn't seem to care. "So why *are* you here, anyway?"

"Because Martin Dalrymple has been murdered."

Chapter Four

Though Alexander Quinn spoke quietly, the apartment was small enough that his voice carried down the hall to Risa's hiding place. She had reached the hallway when she heard his words about Martin Dalrymple.

"Dal's dead?"

Connor and Quinn both turned to look at her.

"You look well," Quinn said.

"Yeah, well, you're a pathological liar," she answered, hoping he was lying about Dal as well. "I talked to Dal not long ago."

Except it hadn't really been that recent, had it? He hadn't responded to her last message, which was highly unusual. He might already have been dead by then, she realized, trying to remember the last time she'd actually connected with her boss. It had been early this morning. He'd sent an email, asking her for an update. She hadn't had a chance to respond before her trip to the doctor. And then, afterward, she'd started to feel as if she were being watched.

Had that been Connor's scrutiny she'd been sensing? Or was it something else?

"Dalrymple's body was found this afternoon in Rock Creek Park."

She shook her head. "He wasn't in DC. He said he'd left the city a couple of weeks ago for a more secluded place."

"All I can tell you is what I know. It's Dalrymple. And he's dead."

"You're sure it's murder?" Connor asked.

"Two gunshots to the head. Double tap."

"Execution style," Risa murmured.

"Considering his line of work, most likely."

She pressed her fingertips to her throbbing temples. "I sent him an email earlier today. He never got back to me. I guess now I know why."

"Was it encrypted?" Quinn asked.

"Of course. Agency-level cipher, plus electronic encryption." Her legs felt wobbly. She crossed to one of the chairs at the table, bending forward and taking a couple of deep breaths.

Connor reached her within a second, crouching by her side to look up at her. He rested his hand on her knee. "You okay?"

"I'm fine." She covered his hand with hers. "It's just been a long, stressful day. And now Dal…"

"If the person or persons who killed Dalrymple managed to get their hands on his communications, Risa could be in grave danger," Quinn warned. He'd stayed where he was, near the door. "You should both come back with me to Campbell Cove."

Risa looked up at Quinn. "Where's Campbell Cove?"

"Eastern Kentucky," Connor said quietly. "I work for Campbell Cove Security Services now."

"Your husband signed on with me not long after the plane crash," Quinn added.

"I thought you were running some place called The Gates," she said to Quinn. "Down in Tennessee or somewhere."

"I was," Quinn said. "I still own the place. But I've trained people there to run The Gates without my day-to-day input. You can say that my country called me back into service."

"So, this is a government agency?" Risa looked at Connor. "I thought you wanted out of that kind of work."

"Technically, it's a government contractor."

"Close enough," she said. "So you changed your mind."

"Circumstances changed my mind." His gaze settled on her face. "You can understand that, can't you?"

She tightened her grip on his hand, wondering how she'd ever thought she could leave him behind, even if it was for his own protection. She'd been miserable without him. Not even the joy of carrying his child had been able to overcome how much she'd missed him.

She'd tried to put him out of her mind, tried to tell herself she had lived most of her life without him, so surely she could live the rest of it without him as well.

But she'd never been able to let him go. Not really. And now that he was here with her again, touching her, gazing at her with those sharp blue eyes that always made her feel deliciously naked and exposed— she couldn't go back. She couldn't walk away again, even for his own safety.

Of course, it was possible that he didn't want her back in his life, after the way she'd betrayed him by letting him believe she was dead.

He stood, pulling his hand away from her grasp. "So, what now?" he asked Quinn.

Quinn looked at Risa. "Is there anything in your apartment you need?"

"My gun and my computer. A couple of changes of clothes would be good, too. Everything else is in my purse." She nodded toward the shoulder bag sitting on the table next to her.

"I'll go get her things," Connor volunteered.

"No. You'd raise too many eyebrows. I'll go get what I need." She pushed to her feet, trying not to grimace at the ache in her back and thighs.

"You've been on your feet all day," Connor protested.

"Let her do this," Quinn said quietly. "She's the one who's been here for months. This is her territory. We're strangers."

"She's not going alone."

"You can wait in the alley behind my apartment building," Risa suggested, grabbing her purse. She pulled a pen and a small notepad from inside and jotted something on one of the pages, tore it out and handed it to Connor. "This is my address. There's a fire escape just outside my window. If anything goes wrong, I'll come down that way. Okay?"

Connor looked from her to Quinn, then back to her again before he nodded. "Okay. Let me at least call you a taxi."

"No." She grabbed the coat she'd draped over one of the chairs and picked up her purse. "People in my neighborhood know I don't make enough money to take taxis. There's a bus that runs past this street in ten minutes. I'll catch it. You can catch it with me, but we have to act like strangers. You can't sit with me or talk to me."

Connor's brow furrowed and his mouth tightened, but he nodded.

"I'll wait here," Quinn said, settling in the chair by the window. He tilted it back on two legs and tapped his watch. "Nine minutes now. Better get a move on."

"I'll go first." Risa finished buttoning her coat and started toward the door. "Wait a couple of minutes, then you come down after me. I'll be waiting at the bus stop. And you should get off at the stop before my street. It's the one on Vine, near Washington Park. I assume you can find my place from there."

"Of course," he agreed.

She slipped out the front door, her heart already starting to race. Logically, she knew that she was probably as safe now as she had been before she'd learned the news of Dal's death. He had been a target long before he'd sent her to Cincinnati, and the people who killed him probably had no idea how many different missions he had running at any given time.

He could have been killed for one of those other missions, not hers.

But as she reached the street and walked the half block to the bus stop, she couldn't help feeling as if she had an enormous neon target on her back. Those Kaziri men had seen her outside the building they'd entered. From a distance, yes, on a dark street, but had they seen enough to make it easy for them to recognize her if they saw her again?

What if they were already asking questions around the neighborhood, trying to figure out who the pregnant woman in the dark *roosari* might be?

Stop it, she admonished herself. They probably hadn't gotten a good look at her at all. And she'd been wearing her coat, which might have hidden her pregnant belly well enough in the dark at that distance.

She would go home the way she normally did. If she'd worked her full shift, and maybe stayed behind to help with the after-hours cleanup, she wouldn't be home much earlier than now anyway.

Everything was going to be fine.

"You must feel as if you're in some sort of surreal dream," Quinn commented in an offhand tone that Connor knew was anything *but* offhand.

"You're not seriously going to try to shrink me now, are you?" Connor zipped his jacket and turned to look at his boss. "Because you would surely know that trying to handle me that way would just royally piss me off."

"You just found out your dead wife is alive and

carrying your baby. That's not something you can train for."

"I've got five minutes to get down to the bus stop before I miss my ride. Let's not talk about this now. Or ever."

Quinn lifted his hands with a shrug of surrender. "Don't stay out too late, McGinnis. Time isn't on your side."

Quelling the urge to throw something at the man, Connor opened his door. "I'll be back soon. Don't touch any of my stuff. I *will* know if you do."

The night had managed to grow even more bitterly cold, making him wish he'd added another layer of clothing beneath his leather jacket before he left the apartment. He spotted Risa sitting on the concrete bench situated near the bus-stop sign on the corner, her slender arms wrapped around herself as if to ward off the cold. Her wool coat looked as if it had come out of a charity bin, the material thin in places and appearing ill-equipped to protect her from the cold wind. She'd donned the *roosari* again, he saw. Playing the part of the Kaziri widow.

He kept his distance, as they'd agreed, not even sharing more than a glance with her. But the forced separation only served to make him more aware of her than ever.

And with the awareness came a gut-twisting sense of anxiety that if he turned his head too far and lost sight of her even in the corner of his eye, she'd disappear from his life again, gone forever.

The sight of the blue-and-white Metro bus came

as a relief. With a faint squeal of brakes, the bus lumbered to a stop and idled with a low grumble as Risa put her money in the fare box and took a seat near the exit door in the middle of the bus.

Connor paid his own fare and sat on the opposite side of the bus, a few seats back from her. They were among only a handful of riders on the bus at this time of night, most of them young. The pretty African American girl who sat across the aisle from him appeared to be a student, her well-used backpack sitting on the seat beside her while she pored through a large history book spread out on her lap.

Two olive-skinned men in their early twenties sat together a couple of seats ahead of Risa. The one on the aisle turned to look at her, his expression full of disdain.

When he spoke, it was in Kaziri, his tone low and mean. "Are you a whore?"

Risa's back stiffened, but she didn't respond.

The man who sat with him turned to see who his friend was talking to. His brow furrowed, though more in concern than disdain. "Does your father allow you to travel at night alone?" he asked in English.

"I am here alone," Risa answered in heavily accented English. "I have no father to protect me. Please, leave me be."

"Your child has no father?" the first man asked.

"Leave her alone." The studious girl had put down her book and now stood, glaring at the two men across the column of seats. "Those questions aren't your business."

The young man who'd spoken to Risa with concern looked embarrassed and turned quickly toward the front of the bus, but the other man glared at the student for a moment before he turned around and started speaking in low tones with his friend.

Risa turned to the young woman. "Thank you," she said softly.

The student moved her backpack to the floor of the bus and patted the seat beside her. "You can come sit with me if you want."

Risa glanced across at Connor for a brief second before she rose and joined the student across the aisle.

"I'm Kyla," the girl said with a friendly smile.

"Yasmin."

"Nice to meet you."

Though Connor tried to look relaxed and uninterested, he kept one ear open to their small talk while he kept both eyes on the young men at the front of the bus. Fortunately, they exited at the next stop and he was able to drop his guard a little until he reached his own stop.

He wished now he hadn't agreed to get off first. He should have let her exit the bus first, and then get off at the following stop. But the plan was already under way, so he got off the bus when it pulled to a halt and started down the block toward the address Risa had given him.

He'd entered the location on his phone before he

left his place. Now he followed the directions, moving at a brisk jog along the mostly deserted sidewalks. As he neared the corner of her block and made the turn, he saw the bus pulling away from the curb.

Risa was walking toward him, her head lowered against the wind. She slowed when she reached the front stoop of a shabby three-story brownstone building in the middle of the block. As she opened the front door, she lifted her gaze to meet his. She didn't show any sign of recognition, only moved a little more quickly into the building.

She'd told him there was an alley between her apartment building and the next. He found the darkened breezeway, which was little more than a footpath between the buildings. Overhead, alternating fire escapes created an open-air canopy that offered no shelter but some small measure of concealment in the darkness.

Her apartment was on the second floor, in the corner facing the alley. Leaning against the cold brick of the opposite building, he fixed his gaze on the dark window, waiting for light as he counted the seconds. Ten. Twenty. Thirty.

There. A light appeared in the window.

He let himself breathe again.

RISA HAD NO idea where she was supposed to sleep in Connor's half-empty apartment, but she didn't particularly care. She was tired enough to curl up in a corner on a spare towel and sleep for a week.

But first, she had to grab anything that a nosy landlord might find that would suggest she was anyone but the pregnant widow she'd portrayed for the past seven months. Her disappearance was going to raise enough eyebrows as it was.

Dal had supplied her with a backpack in which to hide the laptop and other communications equipment he'd provided for her. The exterior of the pack looked old and well-used, concealing all signs of the expensive equipment inside. She stuffed a few changes of clothing and all of her toiletries in a gym bag she'd picked up on her own at a discount store. Anything she didn't think she'd need, she left behind, along with the cash she'd saved up to pay the next month's rent.

Going from room to room, she checked behind doors and under furniture to make sure she hadn't forgotten anything that might give someone any clues to her real identity. The apartment was small, but over the past seven months, she realized, she'd turned it into something of a home.

But her life here had never been anything more than a facade. Yasmin Hamani was a mask she'd worn to protect herself and her child.

And to protect Connor as well, though she didn't think he could see her choice that way. Not yet.

Maybe not ever.

Finally satisfied she'd left nothing of importance behind, she shouldered the heavy backpack, gripped the duffel bag in one hand and unlocked her front door. After one last backward glance, she turned out the lights and shut the door behind her.

She had made it only a few steps into the stairwell when she heard a man speaking Kaziri. His words drifted up from the first floor. "You are sure this is the place?"

Daring a quick glance over the railing to the floor below, she saw a flash of bright embroidery as the wearer headed up the steps.

It was one of the Kaziri men she'd followed from the restaurant. What was he doing here, of all places?

A second voice, even more familiar, answered her question as well as the Kaziri man's. "This is the address she gave when she took the job," Farid Rahimi answered, his tone surprisingly reluctant. "Why do you want to see her? She is nobody. A poor widow."

Damn it. They were talking about her.

There was another set of stairs at the far end of the hall, but she'd never reach them before the men arrived on her floor. Instead, she scurried back into her apartment and locked the door behind her.

She left the lights off, hoping they might think she was still out. But the person who knocked on the door wasn't Farid or the Kaziri customer.

"Mrs. Hamani? Are you home?"

The voice on the other side of the door was Joe Trammel, her landlord.

And he had a key.

Tamping down a burst of adrenaline, she backed deeper into the small apartment, toward the bedroom.

She could hide in the closet or under the bed. Surely they wouldn't do a thorough search of the place with Mr. Trammel there watching.

She heard the rattle of keys in the front door and hunkered down by the bed, ready to slide under it. But the bulge of her belly, pressing hard against her chest, caught her by surprise.

Damn it. No way could she get her pregnant belly under that bed.

She stood and moved toward the closet, listening for a voice in the front room. Joe Trammel spoke first, his voice loud and a little impatient. "Maybe she didn't realize she was supposed to work tonight, ever think of that?"

Farid must have lied to the landlord, told him she hadn't shown up for work. Damn it.

"She is one of my best workers," Farid answered. "She would not miss work. Something may be terribly wrong with her. Maybe her baby has come?"

Trammel sounded faintly horrified. "You think?"

"We will check now, yes?" That was the other man, the one who'd looked familiar to Risa. He spoke with a flawless British accent, as if he'd been schooled there. Which, she supposed, wasn't at all unusual in the world of terrorism these days.

"It's just—I was just about to run out and pick up my wife from work," Trammel said. "I don't want to leave her out there in the cold waiting—"

"You go pick up your wife." Farid spoke in his most appeasing "the customer is always right" tone of voice. "I will stay here until you get back. Perhaps Yasmin will return and all will be well. But if she doesn't, and I find anything troubling, we can decide if we should call the police when you get back. It's a good plan, yes?"

"All right," Trammel said, although Risa heard a hint of unease in his tone. But apparently he overcame the doubt, his heavy footsteps moving away from the apartment.

Risa's heart sank. Now she was alone with Farid and the mystery man. Not good odds. Not good at all.

She had to get out of here.

Hearing them moving around out in the front room, she made her move, easing the lower sash of the window silently upward. One of the first things she'd done upon moving into the apartment was make sure the window sash that opened onto the fire escape could be raised without effort—or sound. She'd just hoped she'd never have reason to make a quiet escape.

She should have known better.

Icy air poured into the room as she lifted her duffel and backpack over the sill and out onto the fire escape outside. As she started to follow, she heard Farid and the other man approaching the bedroom and froze. The men conversed in Kaziri, their voices almost too quiet to make out. She heard words more than sentences—"strange woman" and "surveillance" made it to where she waited by the window.

Their voices came nearer, moving down the hallway. This time, a full sentence came through, loud and clear, from the Kaziri man she'd tried to follow earlier in the evening. "Could she be a spy?"

"Yasmin? No. She is a meek little mouse," Farid answered.

"Mice can do great damage," the other man said grimly.

Risa heard footsteps just outside her bedroom door. She didn't wait for them to enter, stepping out onto the fire escape, her heart in her throat.

Chapter Five

The light in the apartment had gone out a couple of minutes ago, and Connor had breathed a sigh of relief, expecting Risa to appear in the alley any minute. But the light in the window had appeared again moments later.

Had she forgotten something?

Or had she planned all along to ditch him?

As he pushed himself away from the wall, the faint creak of metal scraping against metal made him freeze in place. Moving only his eyes, he looked up at Risa's window and saw a shadowy figure silhouetted briefly against the light in the window. Then, with a soft rattle of iron, the figure dropped the fire escape ladder and began to descend.

It was Risa.

Connor hurried over to the lowered ladder, holding his breath as she started climbing down, her descent encumbered by the small duffel bag and backpack dangling from her arms.

She looked down at him, fear glinting in her eyes.

"Take the bags," she hissed, letting them drop into his outstretched hands one at a time.

He caught the bags and put them on the ground, then reached up to help her the rest of the way down. Even carrying the extra weight of the baby, she felt fragile and light.

Breakable.

He'd never thought of her as breakable before.

"My boss and one of those two men from the diner tricked my landlord into letting them in my apartment." Her voice was barely a breath in his ear. "Let's get out of here. Fast, before they spot us."

He pushed her ahead of him and grabbed the bags. The backpack was as heavy as it had felt when he caught it, making him wonder what it contained. Her laptop? Other equipment?

What kind of operation had she and Dal been running?

At the end of the alley, he dared a glance back. Spotting a man's head lean forward to look out the window, he hurried around the corner of the building, hoping they'd made it out of sight in time.

"What excuse did they give the landlord to get inside?" he asked Risa as he caught up to her. She was walking ahead of him, moving at a surprisingly quick clip after the stressful, tiring day she'd just lived.

"Welfare check, from what I heard. My boss must have lied and said I didn't show for work. I guess, since I'm pregnant, it was enough to make my landlord worry that I might be in trouble." She darted a look behind them. "There's a bus stop two blocks this way."

She started across the empty street, leaving him to follow.

They reached the bus stop in five minutes. "There should be one more bus scheduled tonight," she told him.

"Are you sure?"

She slanted a look up at him, a slight smile curving her lips. "I checked the bus schedule online before I packed up my computer. In case we needed to make a fast getaway."

Resourceful, he thought. That was Risa.

He felt a familiar tug low in his gut, a pull of attraction and admiration and awe, all wrapped up in one small, brilliant woman. And then, like a slow rolling detonation, the delayed impact of the reality he'd been tamping down beneath his game face finally hit him with devastating force.

She's alive.

Shock waves of pent-up emotion blew through him, and he ended up dropping to the cold bus-stop bench before his knees buckled.

He took several deep breaths, his heart hammering as if he'd run for miles. Risa sat, her compact body warm beside him, and she put her hand on his arm.

"What's wrong?"

How could he tell her what he was feeling when he couldn't trust the emotions? Yes, he was thrilled beyond words that she was alive. He had mourned her deeply, longed for her when she was no longer within his reach, but those feelings seemed to belong to another person.

A person who couldn't have imagined that his wife would let him believe she was dead when she was very much alive.

And carrying his child.

He forced himself to leash those dangerous feelings again, pack them away in the rucksack of his self-control. "Nothing," he answered, already feeling his body coming back under control, his heart rate subsiding and his breathing resuming a normal cadence.

Risa's eyes narrowed as if she knew better, but she didn't push. She just turned her face back toward the street. "There's the bus."

There was little point in sitting apart on the nearly empty bus. In retrieving her things from her apartment, Risa had closed the door on the pregnant Kaziri widow named Yasmin Hamani. She sat close to Connor one row back from the side door of the bus, where they could keep an eye on anyone entering or exiting the bus until they'd reached his apartment.

"I guess we need to discuss sleeping arrangements," Risa murmured. Now that she'd stopped using the Kaziri accent she'd affected for her undercover work, her Georgia drawl was back, all sweet honeysuckle and sultry humidity.

Desire gnawed low in his belly, but he made himself ignore it. "I have a sleeping bag I can use until we can arrange something else."

She slanted a narrow-eyed look at him but said

nothing more, and they passed the next few minutes in silence.

They exited the Metro bus about two blocks from the walk-up he was renting. Risa released a soft sigh as she looked up the stairs, but she trudged upward without complaint, waiting for him to catch up.

Quinn was still there when they entered the apartment, waiting in the chair by the window. He sat facing the door, watching calmly as they entered. "I take it the op went well?" His tone was dry and slightly amused.

"Not exactly." Risa sank onto one of the chairs by the table and stretched her legs out in front of her. She rolled her neck side to side and flexed her back, her eyes closing with concentration, as if she could somehow will away the tiredness.

Connor took two strides toward her before he caught himself, remembering that seven long, painful months had passed since he'd last given her a foot rub. They weren't the same people anymore.

He didn't know if they ever could be again.

He changed course, walking to the window. "Risa's boss at the restaurant and one of the men she followed tonight talked their way into searching her apartment."

Quinn rose in alarm. "While she was there? Did he see her?"

"She was in the apartment, but she went out the bedroom window. Took the fire escape down to the alley and we left that way. I'm not sure if the guy saw us or not. It was dark. At most, he might have gotten a glimpse of me."

Quinn's gaze moved to where Risa sat slumped in her chair. "You need to get out of Cincinnati," he said to Connor.

"But the assignment—"

"Can be covered by another operative," Quinn finished firmly. "You need to get Risa out of here and to one of our safe houses in the hills."

By hills, Connor knew, Quinn meant the mountains of eastern Kentucky, where the security company was located. There were hollows and coves in those hills where a man could get lost forever, by accident or by choice.

"I don't think anyone here has figured out who I really am," Risa said. Even her honeysuckle drawl sounded bone-tired. "And if you think I'm going to go anywhere else tonight after the day I've had—"

"It's a four-hour drive in a comfortable Chevy Tahoe. Heated reclining seats, satellite radio—" Quinn pulled a set of keys from his pocket. "I'll stay here tonight, in case anyone comes calling. Leave me your car keys, McGinnis."

Risa looked at Connor, as if asking his opinion.

"I think we should go tonight," he told her. "If those guys are suspicious of you, they're going to keep looking into who you are. And if they find out you're still alive—"

"Dal was trying to figure out who had put the hit on me." A flicker of pain passed through her weary expression. "Now he's dead. And I don't know what he found out."

"We have people looking into that homicide investigation," Quinn said. "I can keep you apprised."

"This safe house—are we going to have armed guards there?"

"No. We'll just provide you with extra weapons." Quinn's eyes sparked with wry amusement. "You're both capable of protecting yourselves, and the smaller the footprint, the better."

"So we'll be all alone. Just the two of us." Risa's gaze met Connor's. Tension coiled low in his belly at the thought.

"Weren't you going to be alone together here tonight anyway? At least there, you'll actually have furniture." Quinn traded keys with Connor. If he was aware of the sudden rise of tension in the room, he didn't comment. "We'll have a regular schedule of check-ins. Don't worry. Just get there tonight. Settle in. Someone will be in touch."

RISA WOKE TO the sound of windshield wiper blades swishing in a steady rhythm. Otherwise, the cab of the large black SUV was quiet. As she pulled her reclined seat upright, Connor glanced her way. "Started snowing again about an hour ago. It's going to add some time to the drive."

She rubbed her gritty eyes and looked through the windshield, where the Tahoe's headlights illuminated a thick flurry of falling snow that had already begun sticking to the road in slick patches. "How far out are we now?"

"Maybe an hour."

The clock on the dashboard read four thirty. They had already been on the road for more than the four promised hours. "You sure we can drive up a mountain in this weather?"

"Four-wheel drive. Quinn says we'll make it."

Quinn says, she thought, *and people believe*. The man had never been part of her unit when they were both in the CIA, but she knew enough of his reputation to recognize he'd earned at least some of the belief people placed in his wisdom and knowledge.

But she also knew enough about life in the CIA to know that he'd speak with authority on subjects he knew little about if he thought it would get the job done.

"You don't like Quinn," Connor commented, as if reading her thoughts. He used to be ridiculously good at reading her, she remembered. It had been terrifying on one level, and deeply comforting on another. To be known so well, to be understood—

How could she have let Dal convince her she had to let go of Connor after the plane crash? Was he in any less danger if people thought she was dead? Connor had been a marine. He faced death daily in his work, and even now that he was out of the Corps, he still seemed to be working a job that came with its own share of danger.

She hadn't spared him anything at all. And she

could imagine the pain she'd inflicted on him by letting him believe she was dead.

If she'd thought he was dead, she'd have been utterly devastated.

"I'm sorry, Connor."

He slanted a quick look her way before concentrating on the deteriorating weather conditions outside the SUV. "For what?"

"I made a terrible decision. I get it now."

"Hindsight and all that," he said, his tone free of emotion.

"You're never going to forgive me, are you?"

"Risa, we're tired. We're driving in snow and we're going to a strange place so that people we don't know can't find us. It's taking every ounce of my remaining consciousness to keep this behemoth of a vehicle on this slick road. Let's just get to the safe house and get some sleep. We can hang out all our dirty laundry tomorrow, okay?"

"Fine." She swallowed the anger that rose in her chest at his weary tone, reminding herself that she was the one who'd made the mistake, not Connor. She owed him a little patience and forgiveness of her own, even when his unemotional handling of this crazy situation made her wonder if he'd ever really loved her at all.

The safe house turned out to be a small farmhouse of clapboard and river stone in the mountains northeast of Cumberland, Kentucky. The narrow, winding road to the safe house was paved with gravel, and while by the time they reached the road, snow had hidden most of the loose stones from view, the *snap-pop* of the Tahoe's tires on the loosely packed gravel gave away their presence.

The house itself was hidden from view for most of the journey, appearing suddenly as the road took a bend along the banks of a large creek. A narrow iron bridge spanned the creek, acting as a driveway for the house, which lay not far from the bridge's end.

"Quinn says there's a key to the house hidden in one of the foundation stones near the back stoop," Connor said as they parked the SUV out of sight behind the house.

Risa eyed the hundreds of stones that made up the house's foundation. "That's helpful."

"Stay in here where it's warm and dry. I'll see if I can find it." Connor stepped out of the SUV, leaving the engine running for heat. Risa might normally have insisted on joining him in the key search, two sets of eyes being better than one, but she was tired, her back was aching, and going out in the snow probably wouldn't be good for the baby.

Connor turned around, finally, holding up something shiny. She thought he even cracked a smile before he climbed the three low steps of the back stoop and unlocked the door, but that might have been wishful thinking, for when he came back to the vehicle, his deadpan expression was firmly back in place.

"Quinn must have called someone to let them know we were coming," he told her as he helped her out of the passenger seat. "The heat and electricity are on, and there's a fire laid in the hearth just waiting for a match."

"I need a bathroom and a half gallon of water, in that order," she said as he grabbed their bags from the back of the Tahoe. As she started up the short path to the house, he hurried to her side, cupping one hand under her elbow.

"Careful, it's slick out here." He helped her up the stairs and into the house, then went back out to get the rest of their bags.

The back door opened into a small, clean kitchen. Connor had turned on the lights, which shed a warm glow over the Formica countertops and steel appliances. This part of the house, at least, was blessedly warm.

"Any chance the fridge is stocked?" she wondered aloud as Connor brought the rest of the bags inside.

His gaze dropped to her round belly. "You and the munchkin are hungry, huh?"

"Yes, but mostly I'm thinking about later this morning when it's time for breakfast."

"Well, let's check." He opened the refrigerator, revealing that it was partially stocked. There were a couple of cartons of eggs, both with expiration dates several days away. The gallon of milk was also new, and in the freezer, there were several frozen dinners, frozen fruit, a couple of fish fillets wrapped in butcher paper and cellophane, and a pint of chocolate ice cream.

It was the ice cream that made Risa's stomach

growl. As if in response to the rumbling sound, the baby started to kick wildly against her abdomen.

On impulse, she shut the freezer door and grabbed Connor's hand, placing it on the swell of her belly. "Feel that?"

His hand went tense beneath her touch and he frowned. Then the baby gave another hefty kick and Connor's gaze snapped up to meet hers. "Was that the baby?"

She smiled at his thunderstruck expression. "Yeah. That's him. Or her."

"How far along are you?" He moved his hand lightly over her belly, as if willing the baby to kick again.

"A little over eight months. About thirty-seven weeks. Not long now."

Connor dropped his hand from her belly and looked around the small kitchen, his brow knotting with dismay. "And you're stuck out here in the middle of nowhere."

"We have a vehicle. We're not that far from civilization, are we?"

He shook his head, though his expression showed no sign of relaxing. "I think we're maybe ten minutes northeast of Cumberland."

"So we just get online in the morning and figure out where the closest ob-gyn can be found."

"Assuming there's a way we can get online here," he muttered.

"We have phones." She put her hand on his arm. "It's all right, Connor. Women have been having babies for years, and some of them do it without a doctor in sight. Plus, I'm still nearly four weeks away from my due date, and since it's my first baby, I might even be a week late. We don't have to worry about this tonight. Okay?"

He looked at her hand on his arm. "And you've been going through this all by yourself for seven months?"

"I had Dal to talk to." She dropped her hand away, not wanting him to feel sorry for her. She had made the decision to handle the danger hanging over her head the way she had, hidden and alone.

Her choice. Her consequences.

WHEN RISA EMERGED from the bathroom, her hair was wet. She'd taken a bag into the bathroom with her and had changed into soft cotton pajamas obviously cut to accommodate her pregnancy.

Connor watched, mesmerized, as she entered the den where he'd started a blazing fire to ward off the cold. Outside, snow had begun to fall in earnest, already covering the ground outside with a fluffy blanket of white. He'd tried checking the weather on his phone, but he could barely get a signal, and certainly not one strong enough to sustain an internet connection.

He'd made only a cursory exploration of the rest of the house, enough to see that they seemed to have cable TV, which he hoped might mean there was some sort of cable or DSL connection available for the internet. But he'd worry about that later. He and Risa both needed sleep.

"Feel better?" he asked as she crossed to where he sat in front of the fire.

"Cleaner, anyway." She reached her hands toward the fire, flexing her fingers. "Lovely fire."

Pregnancy suited her, he thought. It softened the angular edges of her face and gave her skin a warm glow that even her weariness couldn't quite extinguish.

And he'd missed most of it, damn it. "I wish I'd known."

He hadn't meant to say the words aloud, but he didn't have to explain what he meant. Risa followed his gaze to her pregnant belly and gave him a regretful look. "I should have told you. I shouldn't have let Dal talk me into trying to handle everything by myself. But it's just—"

"It's how you've always done it. I know. I remember."

She drew her hands away from the fire's heat and twined them together on what was left of her lap. "It wasn't anything to do with us. With you or the way I feel about you. I need you to understand that."

"I do." He knew she loved him. Love had never been an issue between them. "But you can't let go of even a tiny piece of your autonomy, can you?"

"I've had to take care of myself all by myself for a long time. Letting someone else take care of me, take risks for me—"

"Doesn't come naturally."

She leaned her head back against the chair cushion. "I know I've been a disappointment to you."

"Don't do that."

Her eyes, which had drifted shut, snapped open to look at him. "Do what?"

"Turn this around on me. Don't try to make me feel guilty about the way I'm feeling. You're the one who left. You're the one who lied." As the anger and pain he'd been bottling up started to bubble to the surface, he rose from the chair and walked away, needing the distance to get his emotions back under control.

"You're feeling something?" she shot back at him. "That's new. I thought you never let yourself feel anything on a mission."

Her comeback hit painfully close to home. "So this is my mission? And you're what, the client I'm charged to protect? Is that how you want this to go, Risa? Because I'm trained to handle it."

She closed her eyes again, slumping deeper in her chair. "I don't want to dive headfirst into the mess I've made of our marriage right now. Okay? I just want to get some sleep. In the morning, we can rip what's left of it to shreds if you want. But not tonight." She staggered to her feet and headed down the narrow hall, opening the door to one of the two bedrooms and disappearing inside.

Connor stared after her long after the door clicked shut behind her. His gut was burning with restrained emotions, love, anger and pain all wrapped up in a writhing knot in the pit of his stomach.

"You didn't make the mess alone, sweetheart," he whispered.

Chapter Six

Risa woke to the mouthwatering aroma of eggs and toast, but the bedroom was cold enough to give her pause before she finally crawled out from beneath a pile of warm blankets. She dressed quickly in maternity jeans, thick socks and a long-sleeved sweater, and wandered down the hall to the kitchen to find Connor.

"Good. You're up." Connor was at the counter, spreading butter onto a couple of pieces of toast. He waved toward the stools on the other side of the breakfast bar. "Can you drink coffee?"

"I've given it up for now," she said with regret. "The doctor said I could probably have a cup a day, but you know me and coffee. I can't stop at a cup a day."

He gave her a sympathetic wince. "Had to go cold turkey, huh?"

"Yeah." She found herself eyeing him warily as he spooned scrambled eggs onto two plates and added a slice of toast to each. Considering the tension still roiling between them the previous night when she went to bed, Connor seemed awfully chipper. "Did you get any sleep?"

"A couple of hours. I didn't want to sleep too long, though. We have a lot to do today."

She scooped up a forkful of eggs. "We have an agenda for the day, I take it?"

"Well, I do. And I could use your help if you feel up to it. But I can do it alone, at least for a while. If you want to catch up on your sleep."

She glanced at her watch. It was only nine thirty. She'd managed about four hours of sleep. It would have to do. "No, I'm good. What are we doing today?"

"A little mission analysis, I guess you could call it. You and I have been working what seems to me to be two angles of the same investigation. Plus, there's Dal's death and the plane crash earlier this year."

She chewed a bite of toast and thought about what he was saying before she spoke. "For you, it started with that surveillance photo, right? You saw the pregnant Kaziri woman and realized it looked like your dead wife."

"Right." His earlier bright facade slipped a bit.

Imagining what that must have been like for him, she barely kept herself from reaching out to touch him. "That had to have been a real shock."

He ignored the comment. "We think al Adar or some other foreign group—maybe al Qaeda, maybe ISIS—is planning some sort of mass casualty attack. Maybe for the Christmas holidays. But we don't know if it's specifically for Cincinnati, or if they're using Cincinnati as their base of operations."

"Cincinnati doesn't seem as if it would be a big enough target," she said. "They'd want to make a bigger impact, wouldn't they?"

"Maybe. Or maybe they're looking to spread terror out of the bigger cities and into the heartland."

He had a point, she supposed. In the past few years, lower-casualty strikes had already taken place in locations such as an Army base in Texas, a processing plant in Oklahoma and a Navy reserve center in Tennessee. And there was that Christmas party shooting out in California...

Connor picked up his empty plate and took it to the sink. "Those two men from the restaurant—what made you decide to follow them?"

"A couple of things," she said after giving it a thought. "Their flamboyance, for one thing. Most of the people in the Kaziri community try to keep a low profile just out of habit. They came here because of the danger and persecution from al Adar and other jihadi groups, so nobody in the neighborhood likes to stand out. Then here come those two guys, dressed up in their Kaziri finest, throwing their weight around— it was just something out of the ordinary."

"You said there were a couple of things. What was the other?"

"There was something so familiar-looking about one of the men at the diner, and I finally realized why," she said. "Dal used to keep a wall of photos in his office, stuck up on a corkboard. Sort of like most-wanted posters, but in his case, he called them wins. Terrorists who'd been killed or captured."

"And he was one of the people on that wall?"

"I think so. Maybe. It was a glance at a wall months and months ago. And I don't even know his name or anything about him."

"If you're right, this guy clearly wasn't killed. And if he was captured he escaped. Do you know anything about an escaped terrorist?"

"No."

"Neither do I." He leaned back in his chair. "I'll say this about those guys, though. If they're part of a sleeper cell, they're not doing a very good job of blending in."

Also a good point, she had to concede. "What if they're the diversion?"

"To make us keep an eye on the shiny baubles while the real sleepers make their move?"

"Maybe. They sure weren't happy to see me following them, though."

"They were worried enough to get your boss to help them take a look around your apartment."

She rubbed her chin. "Maybe we shouldn't have left Cincinnati. It makes me look as if I have something to hide."

"You do."

"But now I'm in no position to find out who the real sleepers are, if our theory is correct."

"I don't think you were in any position to find out at all." Connor nodded at her mostly empty plate. "You done?"

"Yeah." She handed over the plate. "You think that being a woman automatically puts me in no position to find out anything that might be going on behind the scenes. That's what you meant, right?"

"You weren't just a woman. You were a pregnant woman with no husband, no family, no money and no standing in the community. I don't know what the hell Dal was thinking putting you in that position."

"I think the idea was that, as a woman, I'd be almost invisible. Able to move around without attracting any real concern."

"Maybe if you were a married woman. Or part of an influential family. But nobody was going to talk freely in front of you."

She hated to admit he was right. But he was.

What had Martin Dalrymple been hoping to accomplish by putting her in the middle of the Kaziri community in southern Ohio? Had he had a secret agenda he hadn't lived long enough to reveal?

"What are you thinking?" Connor asked from where he stood at the sink, washing their breakfast dishes.

"I was thinking about Dal," she admitted. "Everything you're saying is true. I wasn't at all the best choice to go undercover in that community if he was looking for information on jihadis. Unless…"

"Unless what?"

She turned in her chair to face him. "What if he thought there was a terrorist threat coming from the female side of the Kaziri community?"

He leaned against the counter. "You mean female jihadis?"

"We know more and more females are getting involved in terrorism."

"Usually as a sidekick to males."

"If we're right about those two obnoxiously chauvinistic Kaziri men being decoys to hide a sleeper cell, what better place to hide their plot than among the women they openly disdain?" She stood up, stretching her back. She had been in the habit of taking a long morning walk since she'd learned she was pregnant, but there was at least four inches of snow on the ground outside, and none of the clothes she currently owned were very practical for tromping around in the snow. "Don't suppose your company has a home gym hidden in this safe house somewhere?"

"Carrying around Junior in there isn't exercise enough?" There was a hint of affection in his voice and an endearing softness in his gaze as it settled on her pregnant belly.

"I'll need my strength when it comes time to give birth."

He came closer, almost close enough to touch, though he kept his hands at his sides. "Have you been preparing for it?"

"Childbirth?"

He nodded.

"Some, yeah."

"Have you taken Lamaze classes?" His tone was uncomfortable, as if he'd brought up a particularly delicate subject.

She stifled a smile. "No, it's not really something that's popular in the Kaziri community. But there's a Kaziri midwife in the neighborhood—I consulted her along with my doctor. And I've done some reading and practicing on my own."

"On your own," he echoed faintly, turning away to look out the window at the snowy side yard.

She joined him at the window. "I didn't know I was pregnant when this all went into motion. By the time I realized it, it was too late to back out."

He inhaled deeply, releasing his breath in a slow whoosh. "How did we get here?"

She didn't have to ask what he meant.

He turned to look at her. "I thought we were happy."

"We were."

"Then how could you have just walked away?"

"Dal convinced me you would be in grave danger if the people trying to kill me had any inkling I was still alive."

"Dal." He growled the word with disdain. "Now Dal's dead and you can't even be sure he was telling you the truth, can you?"

"No," she admitted. "But you know there were things I did in Kaziristan that would have made me a pretty valuable target to al Adar."

"Which means you're still a target. If Dal was telling the truth."

"Yeah." The heat of his body beside hers was both a comfort and a source of intense frustration. Every instinct was screaming at her to put her arms around him and bury her face in his chest, to let him wrap his strong arms around her and remind her that she wasn't alone anymore.

But the "don't touch" vibes he was giving off kept her at arm's length. And reminded her that, in all the ways that mattered, she was still alone.

THEY HAD MET on one of the coldest days of the year in Kaziristan, shivering in the icy wind pouring through the mountain gap to whip through their layers of clothing like a hot knife slicing butter. For the first hour, Connor had thought she was a Kaziri informant, there to guide his unit through the treacherous pass on their way to a top-secret, gravely important meeting between the Marines and one of the most powerful tribal leaders in the country.

American efforts to quell the uprising that once again put the troubled republic at risk of another long, deadly civil war had come down to gaining the support of the tribes. Gulan Mohar's good will could potentially save hundreds, even thousands, of lives.

Connor wasn't a politician. He was a warrior, and it had been his job to stay outside the tribal leader's home with the woman while the brain trust talked to Mohar. As they'd waited, she'd started slanting looks at him around the edges of her *roosari*, curious, sultry glances that had set his heart racing.

Then she'd said something in Kaziri he couldn't understand.

"I don't speak the language," he'd told her in Kaziri, some of the only words he'd known at the time.

"No, you really don't," she'd answered in perfect,

Georgia-accented English, her broad grin making her hazel eyes sparkle like jewels.

He'd been halfway in love with her before they left Mohar's compound and headed back down the mountain to the operating base.

It had taken a while longer, he remembered with a faint smile, to convince her she was in love with him as well.

She sat at the breakfast bar with her laptop, surfing the internet for information, while he searched the refrigerator for something to turn into lunch. They'd found where the cable modem and wireless router were stored, along with written instructions for setting it up and using the equipment. After appeasing Connor's worries by making a list of obstetricians within a thirty-mile radius, Risa had started looking for information on Martin Dalrymple's death.

"There's no public record of exactly how he died," she'd told him after an hour of searches. "I mean, yes, the reports all say he was shot, but the police seem to be treating it as a robbery gone wrong, not an execution."

"You know the cops aren't going to tell the press everything they know. Especially if they suspect a professional hit."

She'd fallen silent but kept searching the web while he went outside to scout their surroundings.

The snow was soft and wet and would probably melt before nightfall, as long as the temperature rose into the forties as the forecast predicted. A melt-off would certainly make it easier to make a fast escape if they needed to. But it would also make it that much easier for someone on their tail to find their way up the mountain to this safe house.

At least they were well armed. Both he and Risa had personal weapons, and the set of keys Quinn had given him included a key to a closet down the hall that contained a couple of rifles, a Mossberg shotgun, and hundreds of rounds of ammunition including .45 ammo he could use in his Ruger and .40 rounds that would fit Risa's Glock 23.

"Why did you join Campbell Cove Security?"

Connor looked up from his refrigerator search to find Risa looking at him from her perch at the breakfast bar. Her head was cocked slightly to one side, her eyes bright with curiosity.

"Since I was already planning to leave the Marine Corps before...the plane crash, I went through with it. But then I needed a job. We'd talked about both of us doing something in security consultation, so when Maddox Heller contacted me to see how I was holding up, I guess he realized I needed something to occupy my mind. He, Quinn and a woman named Rebecca Cameron had started the security company a few months earlier. They had also started an academy for ordinary citizens and civilian law enforcement— teaching them skills and tactics for combatting terrorism in their own communities."

"That's a great idea," she said.

"I know. So when he offered the job. I took it."

"I'm glad you had someone looking out for you."

He wondered if he was ever going to reach the

point where talking about the plane crash and the nightmare afterward, knowing the truth about what had really happened, wouldn't make him angry.

He hadn't reached that point yet.

"Just say it, Connor."

"Say what?"

"Say something. Anything. Tell me you hate me for what I did. Tell me you don't even want to look at me. Just say something, because I know you're furious and it's making me crazy to watch you try to hide it."

Something snapped inside him, and as hard as he tried to hold on to his calm, it slipped like water through his fingers, leaving him shaking. "You left me, Risa!"

"Not willingly."

"How can you say that?" He strode away from her, needing distance, needing to breathe. "You let me think you were dead, Risa. One phone call could have fixed that. One stupid phone call!"

Her face showed signs of starting to crumple, but she fought it off, her chin coming up even as her lips trembled. "I know."

Somehow, her strength of will only infuriated him. "*What* do you know, Risa? Do you know that I used to dream every single night for weeks that you'd shown up, safe and sound? That you showed up on the doorstep of our apartment with a smile, telling me that it was all a mistake, that you never got on the plane in the first place?"

He saw her throat bob as she swallowed hard, but she didn't speak.

"I had that dream for weeks. Months. After a while, I lost track. It was the same thing, over and over. I'd wake up, elated, thrilled that you were alive, that you were with me again, and then I'd turn over and look at that empty, cold space on my bed where you used to lie. And it was like losing you all over again."

Her face had gone pale, and she looked as if she were going to be sick. "I'm sorry, Connor. I made a terrible mistake in judgment."

He couldn't stay in this house a moment longer. Grabbing his jacket from the back of the sofa, he headed for the front door.

"Where are you going?" she called after him.

He didn't answer.

SHE WASN'T GOING to cry. She'd done enough crying a few months ago, when she'd made the decision to become another person and leave her old life behind. There wasn't much point in second-guessing the decision at this point. It was done. She couldn't change it.

But maybe she could change the future. Starting with whatever danger might still be hanging over her head.

And Connor's.

So far, all the online articles she'd found regarding Martin Dalrymple's death had been cursory at best. His body had been found in Rock Creek Park early in the afternoon on the previous day. She tried to remember when she'd last spoken to him in person. Three weeks ago? They'd met at a diner in Covington, Kentucky, so he could give her a photograph of a couple of people of interest he wanted her to watch for.

After that, everything she'd received from Dal had come by encrypted email.

He hadn't responded to the last message she'd sent, which made sense, given that he'd been lying dead in Rock Creek Park.

God, Dal was dead. She didn't even know how to feel about that news. Sad? Of course. But she hadn't really been friends with her old boss, had she? Friendships between colleagues could be a liability in the kind of work she'd done for the past decade. She'd learned that from Martin Dalrymple himself.

Had he ever seen her as anything but a useful implement in his espionage toolbox? Had she ever thought of him as something more than a puppeteer, pulling her strings and positioning her exactly where he needed her?

She rubbed her gritty eyes and refreshed the search engine page, hoping a new article had been added to the queue. Because she couldn't shake the growing certainty that whoever had killed Dalrymple was the real danger hanging over her head.

And if she didn't figure out who'd put a price on her head, and soon, she might not get out of this mess alive.

A WATERY SUN had finally begun to break through the clouds overhead, adding an additional layer of warmth to the rising temperatures that had turned the snow underfoot into slush. In the woods surrounding the safe house, snow slid off pine boughs at regular intervals, hitting the ground with soft whooshing plops. Birds sang in the treetops, and somewhere in the distance, he heard the faint rumble of traffic moving along a nearby highway. But otherwise, the world around Connor remained quiet and still, a stark contrast to the maelstrom of disquiet inside his head.

He had to get his feelings under control. Giving in to his anger only gave the situation power over him.

Gave *her* power over him. And he couldn't afford to let that happen. He'd fought damned hard to escape the abyss of grief and despair he'd fallen into after the plane crash. He couldn't go back to that dark place again, even if it was now awash with anger instead of grief.

Maybe especially because of that.

She had made a mistake. They both had. Thinking they could have any sort of real relationship, being the people they were. He was a warrior. She was a spy. They could, at times, be colleagues of a sort, people who shared the same overarching goal, at least, if not the same tactics.

But they never should have tried to be more than that. Never let a few nights of physical release turn into a reckless, hopeless desire for happily-ever-after. It was doomed to disaster from the start. He understood that now.

Maybe she'd done him a favor, proving it sooner rather than later, before their lives became all tangled up with mortgages and—

And what, McGinnis? And kids?

He rubbed his tired eyes. He was going to be a father. With a woman he didn't trust.

And did he even love her now, knowing how she'd hurt him? Would he ever love her again?

That certainly qualified as a whopper of a tangle, didn't it?

He heard the sound of the door opening behind him and turned to find Risa standing in the open doorway, her arms wrapped around her pregnant belly as if she could protect herself—and the baby—from the cold. "Connor?" she called.

He crossed the crusty yard and headed up the porch steps, nodding for her to get back inside. He shook the snow off his boots and followed her into the house, closing the door behind her. "Is something wrong?"

She turned to look at him, her brow furrowed and a jittery look in her warm hazel eyes. "I found an article online a few minutes ago. With a little more detail about Dal's murder. You know he was found late yesterday afternoon at Rock Creek Park, right?"

Connor nodded.

"Well, the latest article had a quote from the police detective in charge. He said they believed Dal had been dead for at least twenty-four hours before he was found. Maybe even as much as forty-eight."

"So?"

"So, who was it who sent me an email yesterday morning, asking for an update on my mission?"

Chapter Seven

"What do you think it means?"

Risa stopped her pacing to look at Connor, who was watching her from his perch at the breakfast bar. Compared to her own agitation, his calm was preternatural—and downright annoying. "I think it means someone pretending to be Dal has been corresponding with me for at least the past day. Or maybe two."

"How many messages are we talking about?"

"At least two if it was the past twenty-four hours. Five if it's as much as forty-eight."

He nodded at her laptop, still sitting open on the breakfast bar. "Can you show me?"

She crossed to the computer and pulled up her emails. "The most recent one was from yesterday morning. It came in just before I had to leave for my ob-gyn appointment."

He looked over her shoulder. The email program was set up to decrypt the incoming emails from Dal, but even without encryption, Dal used a letter-substitution cipher on all the messages he sent to her. She translated for Connor. "He's asking if I've located the Hawk."

"Who's the Hawk?"

"That is the big question." She sat on the stool beside him. "One of the reasons Dal hid me in Cincinnati was to find the Hawk. According to some of our intelligence sources, the Hawk is in the US, setting up some sort of terrorist attack that will rival that of the attacks of 9/11."

"Never heard that boast before." His tone was dry.

"I know. Every Mohamed Atta wannabe talks up his big plot as if it's the next coming of the attack on the Twin Towers. But Dal seemed to think this latest intel was legit and needed to be investigated."

"So he sent you? A pregnant dead woman?"

She worried her lower lip between her teeth, wondering if she should tell him what she suspected about Dal's operation. There wasn't any reason to keep it secret at this point, was there? Dal was dead and she was nearly five hours away from Cincinnati and unlikely to go back there any time soon.

"What aren't you telling me?" Connor's tone was neutral, even relaxed, but she saw a wariness in his blue eyes that made her heart ache.

She'd put that wariness there. Earned it fair and square.

"I don't think Dal was running this operation with official sanction," she said.

"Meaning?"

She wished she didn't have to admit this to Connor, on top of all the other reasons he had to hate what she'd done to him. But if she ever wanted to find her way back into Connor's heart, she had to stop lying to him.

She took a deep breath and said, "I think the CIA believes I'm dead, too. I don't think they know what Dal was doing."

BRIGHT DAYLIGHT POURED through the window of Alexander Quinn's office, the afternoon sun glinting off the melting snow. Campbell Cove Security might be a high-tech government-contracted security facility on the inside, but the outside looked like the sprawling brick and concrete high school it had once been, nestled in the little town of Campbell Cove just a few miles east of Cumberland, Kentucky—and about a fifteen-minute drive from the safe house where he'd sent Connor and Risa McGinnis.

He wondered if they were feeling as tired as he was. He was getting a little too old to run these overnight covert operations without feeling the consequences.

The door to his office opened without a warning knock, and two people entered without hesitation or preamble. One was a sandy-haired man in his early forties, with blue eyes and a golden tan that seemed to have lingered from the years he spent bumming around the Caribbean. The other was a slender, handsome woman in her midforties, with golden-brown skin that showed little of her age, black hair worn in a short, neat cut and sharp brown eyes that missed nothing. They were Maddox Heller and Rebecca Cameron, the closest thing he had to partners.

Over the years, Quinn had learned that he wasn't really partner material.

"We need to talk, Quinn," Cameron said.

"About what, Becky?" He was taking his life in his hands, using her nickname without being asked to do so. Only her close friends called her Becky, and along with being a lousy partner, he wasn't exactly great at being a friend, either.

"What's this about you going to Cincinnati last night?" Heller asked flatly, pulling up one of the chairs in front of Quinn's desk.

Quinn arched one eyebrow. "Have a seat."

"Are you running an op without consulting us?" Cameron asked.

"No," he said. "It's not my op."

"Then whose?" Heller asked.

"Martin Dalrymple's."

"The dead spook?"

Quinn slanted a hard look at Heller. "Martin Dalrymple served this country with honor and distinction, at great sacrifice to himself. A little respect for a fallen hero, please."

Heller looked suitably repentant. "Was he in contact with you?"

"Not exactly." Quinn unlocked the lap drawer of his desk and withdrew a phone he kept locked away most of the time. It was a burner, a phone not even his partners had the number for. It was for old contacts from his days in the agency. Martin Dalrymple had been one of those contacts. "I got a text message from Martin two days ago. It was a code we'd used years ago on another op. He knew I'd remember it."

Cameron's shapely brows lowered, carving a couple of small lines in the smooth skin over her nose. "What kind of message?"

"It said, 'Get her out.'"

"And you knew he was talking about Risa?"

"I'd contacted Dal when we spotted Risa in that surveillance photo," Quinn said. "I asked if he was running an op with her."

"What did he say?"

"He never replied—until that text message."

"So you have no idea what he was up to?" Cameron asked, her curiosity apparently beginning to overcome her irritation with Quinn.

"I'm hoping Risa McGinnis can fill in some of the blanks," Quinn answered calmly. "But I imagine she's skittish at the moment, so we're going to let her calm down and feel safe again before we approach her."

"She won't talk to you," Heller warned. "She ain't stupid."

Quinn looked across the desk at Heller, then turned his gaze to Cameron, taking in her neat-as-a-pin blue business suit, immaculately manicured nails and tasteful, barely-there makeup. Unlike Quinn, the spy, and Heller, the former marine, Rebecca Cameron was all diplomat, which was the role she'd filled for nearly twenty years before a personal loss had driven her out of Foreign Service and into academia. When Quinn had been asked by an old friend to create

Campbell Cove Security and the in-house academy as a resource for the government's war on terrorism, Rebecca Cameron had been one of the first people he'd thought of to bring on board.

She looked like a person who could be trusted. She *was* a person who could be trusted.

"Did you ever meet Risa McGinnis?" he asked Cameron. "Did your paths ever cross while you were in the Foreign Service?"

"No, though I heard about her later, of course. After the plane crash."

Quinn nodded. "She's eight months pregnant. She could probably use another woman to talk to."

Cameron's dark eyes narrowed. "What are you up to, Quinn?"

"Dal's been murdered. Risa may be a target. And meanwhile, we're hearing sporadic chatter from known and suspected terror groups suggesting there's something in the works for the US." Quinn leaned forward, folding his hands in front of him and gazing at his partners across the desk. "If we can stop it, we'll get more assignments in the future."

"This is about money?" Heller stared at Quinn with a look of disgusted disbelief, but Cameron, Quinn noted, had a more thoughtful look on her face.

"I have all the money I need," Quinn said simply. "This is about protecting the people of the United States. That's what it's always been about for me. Are we clear?"

Cameron inclined her head in answer. Heller just pressed his lips together and gave a gruff nod.

"Cameron, I want you to make contact with Mc-Ginnis after lunch. Use a burner phone, just in case. See if there's anything they need." Quinn looked at Heller. "I want you to go to Cincinnati, Mad Dog," using the former marine's old service nickname. "Ask about renting a room in the building where Risa was living. And visit The Jewel of Tablis for lunch. Keep your ears open. I want to know if people are talking about her sudden disappearance."

"Will do."

Quinn waited until his partners left the office before he picked up his own burner phone and made a call to an old friend. "It's me."

On the other end of the line, a smooth baritone answered him with a mixture of pleasure and wariness. "What's up this time, Quinn?"

"I need to know everything you can tell me about Martin Dalrymple."

THE WANING COLORS of sunset clung to the western sky as if unwilling to let go of the day, but what heat the sun had offered was long gone, and to ward off the cold, Risa curled up with her laptop in one of the armchairs next to the fireplace, leaving Connor to come up with something for dinner.

Risa had always been an indifferent cook, happy to let him claim the kitchen in exchange for handling the cleaning and laundry duties. She'd already washed a load of clothes earlier that afternoon, returning from the small laundry room off the kitchen to inform him she was in the mood for eggs and toast for dinner.

He scrambled eggs for their evening meal, adding cheese and onions for a little extra flavor, and toasted the bread in the oven so he could melt butter on top while it was browning. He'd found some frozen strawberries in the freezer and thawed them so that she could get a serving of fruit to go with the carbs and protein.

"Tomorrow," he told her when he brought her plate of food into the living room and set it on the table by her chair, "I need to go into town and find a grocery store. We need better food choices."

She set aside her laptop and picked up the plate. "Cheesy eggs with onion. Do you know how many times I tried to replicate this dish over the past few months?"

"No. How many times?"

"At least two dozen before I gave up. I'm a complete loss in the kitchen."

"You're too impatient," he said, allowing himself a smile as he remembered her whirlwind style of cooking. "Good food requires patience."

She scooped up a forkful of eggs and took a bite. Her eyes rolled back and she gave a moan of pleasure that seemed to rumble through Connor's body like an earthquake, finally settling in a low hum of desire in the pit of his belly. He hadn't let go of his anger at her, or his frustration and pain, but he was nowhere near to immune from the passion he'd always felt when she was within reach.

He set his plate on the fireplace mantel, moving a short distance away to regain control of his hormones.

"What do you want to drink? We have water, milk and orange juice."

"Milk, please," she said around another mouthful of eggs.

He poured milk for her and water for himself, then returned to the living room. As he sat in the chair beside her, resting his plate on his lap, he congratulated himself on recovering his lost equilibrium.

Mostly.

"So, any progress?" He nodded at the laptop computer lying on the floor at her feet.

"I've started a timeline of Dal's emails to me, trying to see if there's a pattern to them. I was hoping maybe they'll tell me more specifically what he was actually looking for in Cincinnati."

He frowned. "Why didn't he just tell you what he was looking for?"

She cocked her head, her brow furrowed. "You know Dal. That's not how he worked."

"Quinn's the same way." He poked a fork into his eggs, the corner of his mouth quirking. "You know, that explains so much about the CIA."

"There was a method to his madness," she said with a touch of defensiveness. "Sometimes, on an undercover op where there are a lot of unknowns, you try to go in with no preconceptions. Or at least, as few as you can manage. Dal didn't want me to assume anything about the Kaziris I'd be living with. He wanted me to assess them on my own, make my own judgments about them and then write up my observations."

"Do you have copies of those written observations?" Connor asked. Maybe some of the things she had observed could add to some of the incomplete findings of their surveillance operation in Cincinnati.

"Of course. I'll have to decrypt them for you."

He nodded, uncomfortably aware that if she'd been any other operative, he might not have been willing to leave the decryption to her. Instead, he might have taken advantage of their forced proximity to sneak a copy of her notes to Quinn for Spear to decrypt.

But he couldn't seem to function as an operative with Risa, no matter how much she'd hurt him by letting him believe she was dead. She was a lot of things, but she wasn't a traitor to her country.

If she knew anything that could protect the US against a terrorist attack of any sort, she'd share it. He was utterly certain of that.

"Why did your company decide to do surveillance on the Kaziri community in Ohio in the first place?" Having finished off her dinner, she set her plate aside, tucked her legs under her and turned to look at him. Her left hand settled on her belly as if by habit, gently rubbing it the way she might soothe a fussy child. He couldn't seem to drag his gaze away from her hand and the swell of her abdomen.

His child was in there, growing and getting ready to greet the world. A week ago, he'd been all alone without any real hope of having a family again, and now he was about to be a father.

Emotion rose in his throat, choking him. He forced himself to look away and struggled to remember what she'd just asked. "Quinn and Cameron—she's the other partner at Campbell Cove Security— both had contacts in the government who believed that there might be al Adar operatives hiding in the migrant community. The only Kaziri groups seeking work visas in the US in any numbers were the non-Muslims being driven out of the southern part of the country by terrorist attacks on their churches and homes, and the Mahalabi tribe from north of Tablis. We didn't think al Adar spies could easily hide among the Kaziris who settled in the Research Triangle in North Carolina."

"Which left the Mahalabi Muslims who settled in Cincinnati."

"Exactly."

"I think that was probably Dal's reasoning as well," she said with a nod. "He told me I would have to behave as a practicing Muslim in order to fit in."

Her mother's family were Muslims from the Mahalabi tribe, Connor knew, though Nazina DeVille had converted to Christianity a few years before she met Risa's father. It had been her change of faith that had put her and her family in danger in the first place. But Nazina had educated her daughter about Islam so that she would understand the world from which her grandparents, aunts and uncles came.

"You've done it before," Connor said. "In Kaziristan, anyway. Was it harder this time?"

"A little." She shrugged. "It would have been easier if the refugees had come from a different tribe, maybe. The Mahalabis are patriarchal in ways that don't have much to do with religious beliefs, to be honest."

"Most of al Adar come from that tribe, don't they?"

She nodded. "Most. Not all."

"You were in Cincinnati the whole time I thought you were dead?"

"The first month, I stayed with Dal at his hunting lodge in West Virginia."

A flicker of jealousy darted through him. "Just the two of you?"

She flashed him a look of disbelief. "Dal? You're jealous of Dal?"

"I'm not jealous."

"Right." Her lips twitched as if she were going to smile, but the expression died away before it ever really started. "Poor Dal."

"A double tap doesn't really sound like an al Adar style of murder," Connor murmured. "Way too businesslike and not nearly symbolic enough."

"Dal probably had other enemies, as many years as he was in the CIA," Risa said. "It might not have had anything to do with what I was doing in Cincinnati."

"Or maybe what you were doing in Cincinnati had nothing to do with al Adar at all."

Her shapely eyebrows notched upward. "Interesting thought. I suppose it could be a branch of al Qaeda. Or ISIL."

"Maybe. Maybe not." He set his plate on the table on top of hers and turned his chair to face her. "When Quinn recruited me, before I agreed to anything, I did a little research on him and his partners in the company. And something I thought was pretty interesting is that most of his expertise, at least when he was running The Gates, was in domestic terrorism.

Specifically, he spent a lot of time and money disman-
tling a militia group called the Blue Ridge Infantry.
Ever heard of them?"

She shook her head. "No, but most of my career
has been dealing with foreign threats, not internal
ones. It's one reason I've been assuming that whatever I was investigating in Cincinnati had an overseas provenance."

"I'm not saying the Blue Ridge Infantry or any
group like them is behind whatever you were investigating in Cincinnati," Connor added quickly. "I'm just
saying, we can't assume we're looking at a foreign
threat just because both Dal and Quinn are interested
in whatever is going on there. They have—had—their
fingers in other pots."

"Hmm." Risa leaned toward him, the sweet smell
of herbal shampoo wafting toward him, filling his
head with potent memories. "Know what I think?"

"What?" he asked, trying to clear his suddenly
befuddled mind.

"I think we need to have a long talk with your
bosses."

He smiled. "That's good. Because while you were
taking a shower earlier, I got a call from one of my
bosses. She's coming here to talk to us in the morning."

Chapter Eight

So this is Parisa McGinnis. Rebecca Cameron entered the small safe house shortly after nine the following morning, her gaze taking in everything—the cozy fire, the way Connor McGinnis stood slightly in front of his back-from-the-dead wife as if to protect her, and the sharp-eyed gaze of the woman herself, who seemed to be studying Cameron with the same animal wariness with which Cameron was assessing her.

Parisa was smaller, somehow, than she had anticipated, even pregnant. She was only average height, several inches shorter than her tall, broad-shouldered husband. She looked almost delicate, though the unclassified information she'd been able to access about the woman's career suggested she was much tougher than she looked.

"I've heard a great deal about you," she said aloud as she shook the other woman's hand and nodded a greeting to Connor.

"I've heard a few things about you as well," Parisa said with a smile that didn't quite reach her eyes. She had a lovely voice, warm and low, with a drawl that was pure South Georgia. It reminded Cameron of a year she'd spent in Savannah, working on a master's thesis in military history.

She'd met Mitch Cranston there as well, although it had been many more years before she thought of him as anything other than a cocky young marine in town on shore leave who could promise nothing but trouble.

She pushed away the memory of Mitch before it distracted her and took in the look of wary concern in Connor McGinnis's blue eyes. She let her own Alabama accent make an appearance, sensing it might put Parisa at ease. "I hope everything you heard was, if not good, at least interesting."

"I was surprised to hear from you last night. I figured we'd be getting another visit from Quinn," Connor said with his characteristic bluntness.

Unhurriedly, she turned her gaze to him. "Quinn asked me to stand in for him, since he was unable to get away."

"Are you here to appease us or to answer our questions?" Parisa asked.

"May I call you Parisa?"

"Risa," the other woman answered shortly.

"Risa," Cameron said with a smile. "It's a lovely name. I should tell you we were all very pleased to learn you had not died in the plane crash."

"Two hundred and twelve other people did," Risa replied bleakly, waving her hand toward the sitting area of the small living room. There were two armchairs near the fire and a small sofa angled opposite.

Risa and Connor took the chairs, leaving her to sit on the sofa alone.

Clearly she was the one in the hot seat.

She sat, crossing her legs casually and folding her hands on her lap, waiting for one of them to speak.

For a moment, they simply looked her over, as if trying to discern her hidden motives. For once, her motives were exactly what she'd told them. She was here to help them, no matter what their dealings with Alexander Quinn might have otherwise suggested. And she was here to find out what they'd learned, pick their brains about what they might be up against, and figure out how Campbell Cove Security could help them.

Connor was the one who finally broke the increasingly uncomfortable silence. "Why did Quinn send you and not Maddox Heller?"

"Heller is on another assignment. Besides, he's our tactics and training guy. Foreign relations and diplomacy are my areas of expertise," she answered with a smoothness born of years in embassies and consulates around the world, dealing with people even more suspicious than the pair sitting in matching armchairs in front of her. "Quinn suspects, and I concur, that whatever trouble you've become embroiled in probably has its basis in a foreign threat."

"Probably," Risa murmured.

"That doesn't mean we shouldn't consider other possibilities, however." Cameron knew that in a government of a country the size of the US, corruption was inevitable. And the higher the stakes, the greater the risks—and rewards—of playing dirty.

She was doing a little investigation into the Cincinnati situation herself, from a different direction. But that wasn't something Risa and Connor McGinnis needed to know, for the moment at least.

"Would you like a cup of coffee? Or I can probably brew a cup of tea." Risa stood, color rising in her cheeks as if she had suddenly realized she was being a bad hostess. Cameron nearly smiled, recognizing the inbred guilt of a fellow Southerner caught in a moment of bad manners.

"Coffee would be lovely," she said with a smile, belatedly observing the proprieties. "One sugar and a splash of milk if you have it."

While Risa disappeared into the kitchen, Connor leaned closer to her, lowering his voice. "What kind of game is Quinn playing here?"

"I don't think he is," she answered, keeping her voice down as well. "He seems to sincerely want to help your wife uncover and eliminate the threats that drove her to fake her own death."

"Does he have any idea what Martin Dalrymple was trying to uncover in Cincinnati?"

"Beyond the stated desire to stop a terrorist attack? No."

"Not as far as you know," Connor corrected.

Cameron inclined her head in agreement. They both knew that Quinn might have motives on his own that he wasn't willing to share with others. "Not as far as I know."

"What about you? Any thoughts on what Risa's actually up against?"

Rather than reply to a question to which she had no good answer, she smiled at Connor. "We'll get to that when your lovely wife returns. Meanwhile, I've brought supplies for you—groceries, for the most part, and a few first aid supplies and other things you might need. They're in my car in the backseat." She handed him her key fob and nodded toward the door.

His eyebrows arching, Connor took the key fob and headed out the door, just as footsteps coming down the hall signaled the return of his wife.

Risa entered the room with a tray on which sat two steaming cups of coffee. She paused a moment when she saw that Connor wasn't there.

"He's gone outside to fetch some supplies I brought," Cameron explained with a smile. "He'll be right back."

Risa set the tray on the coffee table in front of Cameron, sliding one of the cups toward her. She set the other one in front of the chair Connor had vacated. "I don't believe we've ever met before, have we?" she asked, her tone polite.

Cameron smiled. "No, I believe our paths never crossed during my time in the Foreign Service. But you spent a bit of time in Tablis, didn't you?"

"Yes." Risa settled in her chair, one hand smoothing over her round belly. Cameron tried not to let her gaze linger, but emotion overcame her wisdom for a brief moment, allowing her to look a bit longer than she should, her imagination conjuring up the phantom of an old dream. Motherhood. Marriage. Two things she'd once desired with great intensity.

Two things she no longer considered an option.

"I discussed the matter of your pregnancy with Quinn and Heller," she said aloud, dragging her gaze back up to Risa's face. "We have access to an obstetrician in Lexington who has been vetted and cleared to handle sensitive cases. Our company will cover your medical costs if you need treatment before we figure out how to neutralize the threats against you."

"That's very generous."

Cameron smiled. "Your husband is a valued member of our company. Technically, you'd be covered under his insurance policy anyway. We're just cutting through the red tape."

The door opened and Connor entered carrying two large canvas bags full of groceries. He angled a quick look at Risa. "She brought more ice cream. Including Rocky Road."

"Put it in the freezer before it melts," Cameron suggested.

Connor sighed and headed for the kitchen.

"My sister craved ice cream when she was pregnant. I told her she was a walking cliché, which didn't amuse her." Cameron laughed. "But I thought even if your cravings were different, everybody likes ice cream. So I bought three flavors. I take it you like Rocky Road?"

"Who doesn't?" Risa offered the first genuine smile Cameron had seen since her arrival at the safe house. "Thank you."

"This is all very polite and civilized," Connor interrupted, returning from the kitchen, "but I'd like to know how long we're supposed to hide here in the mountains. Shouldn't we be doing something constructive?"

"Such as?" Cameron asked.

"Maybe someone should go have a talk with Risa's boss at the restaurant in Cincy. Find out why he thought it was okay to let a stranger in her apartment to have a look around."

"Someone is," Cameron said, leaving it at that.

"Farid is a chameleon," Risa said with a grimace. "He's not really religious at all, but he plays the game around some of the true believers so that his business doesn't suffer. With others, he's about as American as they come. He's happy to bow to the tribal pecking order if he thinks it'll win him some approval, but I don't think he'd have been helping that man find me if he thought it was about a terrorist attack."

"So you don't think he's driven by any religious or political beliefs?" Cameron asked.

"He believes in money and power. Period." Risa sighed. "Although, in truth, that's what most of the brains behind al Adar believe in, too. They're not like ISIS, trying to establish a worldwide caliphate. Al Adar uses people's beliefs to manipulate them, but it's not about religion for them. It's about getting control over Kaziristan's oil and mineral resources."

"So Farid could be aligned with al Adar?"

Risa thought about it for a moment, then shook her head. "No, I don't think so. The kind of power he wants is much smaller in scale. He likes being the top dog at the restaurant, but I don't think he'd appreciate the responsibilities of being the top dog in a bigger organization. When someone of real power or import comes into the restaurant, Farid's quick to curry favor. That's not the way of al Adar."

"What about other people in the community? Did you have much interaction with them?"

"Ninety-nine percent of the Kaziris living in Cincinnati are wonderful people. Devout, peaceful people who are horrified by what radicals do in their name."

"We know that," Cameron assured her. "But the one percent—"

"Can do a lot of damage," Risa finished for her. "I know."

"Is it possible that the threat against Risa has nothing to do with any of the terrorist groups normally associated with the Middle East and Central Asia?" Connor asked.

"What do you have in mind?" Cameron asked.

He looked at her, wariness in his blue eyes. Analysis wasn't Connor McGinnis's area of expertise, Cameron knew. He'd joined Campbell Cove Security as an expert in weapons and tactics.

But he would never have been on the company's radar if he hadn't also possessed the intelligence to make smart choices and work out tricky puzzles. Quinn, Heller and Cameron had been tasked with hiring only the best people. They'd taken that calling to heart.

"I'm wondering if there could be another reason why someone wants Risa dead."

"Such as?" Cameron directed the question to Risa.

"I was involved in several delicate operations," Risa admitted, looking uncomfortable. "Some of which are still classified and I can't really talk about."

"Was your cover ever blown?"

"Not that I know of, but maybe it happened without my realizing it. Or maybe someone in the government has loose lips. Wouldn't be the first time."

"What was your role in these operations? Were they personal?"

"Do you mean was I a honey trap?" Risa glanced at Connor, as if gauging his reaction. "Early in my career, yes. A couple of times. But not for the past few years."

"So a man you…charmed as a part of your job isn't likely to be the one who put a hit out on you?"

"No," Risa said firmly. "I know the results of both of those operations, and the men involved aren't in any position to seek revenge."

Connor's eyes slanted toward his wife, but he didn't speak.

"So you tell me then, Risa. Who would want you dead badly enough to kill over two hundred innocent people to make it happen?"

A look of realization flickered across her expression briefly before her brow furrowed. "Oh my God."

"What?" Connor asked.

She turned to look at her husband, her eyes wide.

"Remember when I told you that man at the restaurant looked familiar?"

"Yeah. You said you thought you saw his face on Dal's corkboard."

"I did, but I think I know why his face made an impression." Risa looked at Cameron. "I mean, I can't really be sure. The last time I saw this guy's face, it was a decade ago, at least. He wouldn't look exactly the same."

"Who was he?" Connor asked.

"He was one of the terrorists who was part of the siege on the American Embassy in Tablis about a decade ago. I was assigned to track his movements shortly after the siege ended and he escaped. I managed to discover his whereabouts and alert the Kaziri government of his new identity. He was exiled from Kaziristan after that."

"That sounds like a pretty good motive for revenge," Cameron murmured.

"But see, the thing is, he popped back up a few years ago. In fact, you might want to ask your friend Maddox Heller about him."

"Why's that?" Connor asked.

"Because if I'm not mistaken, Maddox Heller watched him die almost eight years ago."

MADDOX HELLER'S DRAWL rumbled over Rebecca Cameron's cell phone, slightly distorted by the speaker. "At the time, Quinn told me they'd found the body. But you know Quinn's relationship with the truth is distant at best. I talked to him about it before I called you back. Turns out that, technically, the authorities never found his body. There were parts of that building that sank into the ground in a geologically unstable area. The government of Mariposa didn't have the money to do an excavation just to recover a missing body."

"And there's no way Tahir Mahmoud could have survived the explosion?" Connor asked, his stomach muscles tightening as he awaited the response.

Heller took longer to answer than Connor liked. "Since nobody recovered his body, I don't know that I could say there's no way he could have escaped," he said finally. "But it's highly unlikely. And since we haven't had any further sightings of the man…"

Something in Heller's tone made Connor sit up straighter. "Why don't you sound more certain?"

"It's just—remember that photo you sent me last night? From the restaurant?"

Connor glanced at Risa. She sat with her legs curled under her, smoothing both hands rhythmically over the curve of her belly. She looked at him, her brow furrowed.

"Yes," Connor answered. "You said you weren't sure it looked familiar."

"I wasn't. I'm still not. It would almost be impossible."

"What would be impossible?" Risa asked, her tone tight with impatience.

"If I hadn't seen that lab in Mariposa blow up myself, I'd have thought the man you saw at the restaurant was an older Tahir Mahmoud."

Connor looked at Risa. "You said you were part of getting him exiled from the country after the embassy siege. Wouldn't he remember what you looked like?"

"I tracked him anonymously. My cover was a junior-grade pencil pusher at the embassy. He wouldn't have known what I looked like."

"What about the surveillance photos from Cincy?" Connor asked Heller. "Have you looked at all of them?"

"I'm just getting up to speed on this case," Heller admitted. "I'll take a look."

"Do that." Connor looked at Cameron. "Can we get our hands on all the surveillance photos from Cincinnati, too? We've seen the man most recently, so we might be able to spot him more easily."

Her eyes narrowed, but she nodded. "I can arrange that."

"Today?"

She shook her head. "It'll take a while to digitize everything. But I can have them all to you by tomorrow morning. Will that do?"

"Yes. Thank you," Risa said.

"I'll make some calls to some old friends in Mariposa, too," Heller said, sounding subdued. "I'd like to be damn certain Tahir Mahmoud hasn't escaped the grim reaper myself." He hung up.

"I remember the name Tahir Mahmoud from the siege on the embassy in Kaziristan," Connor said as he and Risa walked Cameron to the door. "But I never heard about what happened in Mariposa."

"Because of Mahmoud, Heller's wife, Iris, nearly

died," Cameron told him. "Mahmoud died—allegedly—during an attempt on their lives. Iris barely escaped."

"Eight years is a long time to go to ground without a trace." Risa wrapped her arms around herself, shivering a little as a blast of icy air came through the open door.

"He could very well be dead, you know." Rebecca Cameron put her hand on Risa's arm. "Let me know if you need anything. Anything at all."

"Thank you again."

Cameron took a step back and smiled at them both. "I know things are tense and difficult right now, for a lot of reasons. But remember, this was a Christmas you thought you were both going to spend without each other. And now you're not. That's a blessing, regardless of the circumstances."

She flashed another smile and walked down the porch steps to her car.

Connor gave Risa's elbow a light tug, pulling her back inside the warm house. He closed and locked the door behind them before turning to face her.

"She's right about one thing," Risa said, a faint smile tugging at her lips. "I thought I was going to spend Christmas alone. No tree, no decorations, no Santa down the chimney. It was a lonely prospect."

"You remember last Christmas? When we bought that real tree and spent most of January vacuuming up the needles it shed?" Connor's smile faded when he remembered the rest of the story. How he'd found needles in the carpet for months after the plane crash as well, when they'd served to remind him poignantly of all he'd lost.

Risa put her hand on his arm. "I know you're still angry, and I don't blame you. Not a bit. But can't you at least be happy I'm alive?"

He stared at her, feeling as if she'd just slapped him. "My God, Risa. You know I'm so very grateful that you're alive. No matter what else has happened, you have to know that."

"Then can we just hold on to that for a while? Try not to dwell on the rest of it?" She stepped closer to him, her hand sliding up to his shoulder. "I missed you every single day."

He felt a flutter of anger but pushed it down. Not now. He could be angry later.

Now, he just wanted to be grateful she was here, alive, with him.

"I missed you every single day, too," he admitted.

She rested her cheek against his shoulder. Her belly pressed against his, the sensation strange but somehow perfect. He lifted his hands up her back, letting them settle just above her butt. The pregnancy had given her unexpected curves; he let his hands roam over them lightly, taking in the new shape of her body.

She leaned her head back, looking up at him. "A little more junk in the trunk than you remembered?"

He grinned at her. "I have to admit, your breasts are a delightful surprise, too."

She gave her chest a self-conscious glance. "Not too much?"

He shook his head. "Definitely not."

She reached behind her back and brought his hands around to her belly. "Sweet Pea's kicking again."

He curved his palms over the swell of her belly, feeling the flutter of movement against his hands. "Sweet Pea?"

"I'm trying out nicknames."

"Based on the way Sweet Pea's kicking, Bruiser might be the better name." He ran his fingers lightly over the curve of her belly, feeling her shiver under his touch. She looked up at him, her hazel eyes wide and dark.

He knew that look. He'd loved that look, reveled in the way he could make her long for him with just a touch or the sound of his voice. He'd dreamed of that look after the plane crash, deep in his loneliest nights.

She rose to her toes, lifting her face toward his. It would be the easiest, most natural thing in the world to bend his head and meet her halfway.

If only she hadn't lied.

Risa pulled back. "I'm sorry."

"No, I am," he said, reaching for her. He pulled her into his arms, holding her tightly. "I'm sorry that I've let my hurt feelings get in the way of telling you how damn glad I am you're alive." He pressed his lips to her forehead. "No matter what."

Chapter Nine

"I think I should go back to Cincinnati."

Connor's head shot up, his gaze disbelieving. "Are you insane?"

"I lived there for months, Connor, and nobody bothered me."

"That doesn't mean you could go back now without consequences."

"My rent is paid through the end of the month and I didn't send in a request to end my lease, so it's not like my landlord is going to have rented my room to someone else. My job at The Jewel of Tablis wasn't that great. I could get a different job. Or I could go without a job for a few weeks. It would leave me open to do more snooping around that way."

"Quinn wouldn't have pulled you out of there if he didn't think there was a real threat to your life."

"I think he's proceeding with an overabundance of caution."

"You make it sound like that's a bad thing."

"If it gets in the way of finding out who brought down that flight out of Kaziristan, it *is* a bad thing."

"Risa—" He stopped with a sigh and rose from his crouch by the fire, which he'd been trying to stoke back to life. He crossed to where she lay curled up on the sofa, tucked beneath a warm quilt. Sitting on the coffee table, he took her hand between his. "Your hands are cold."

"Please don't try to talk me out of this, Connor."

"I don't want you to go back to Cincinnati. The thought terrifies me."

"I feel as if I'm walking away from the first real break I had in the case."

"It's not your case anymore. Cameron, Quinn and Heller are on it."

"No, listen, Connor." She squeezed his hand. "I've been thinking about this ever since Cameron left this morning. Dal wouldn't have put me in Cincinnati if he didn't think I was uniquely suited for the investigation."

"But you were there for months and didn't discover a damn thing, did you?" He twined his fingers with hers, leaning closer. He smelled good, crisp and clean with just a hint of wood smoke from the fire, and she felt as if her insides were melting into a gooey mess.

"It was a delicate operation," she protested, annoyed that she couldn't seem to drag her gaze above his mouth. Connor was an amazing kisser, she remembered. Instinctive, knowing when she wanted a soft wooing and when she wanted unbridled passion.

Either would do very nicely at the moment.

But he'd been right to slow things down between them earlier. She wanted him as much as she ever had, and the way his blue eyes dilated with desire when he looked at her told her he felt the same raw longing that she did. But what they both wanted was what they'd had before the plane crash. Before her lies. Before his grief.

Until they could want something else, something built on the future rather than trapped in the past, then it was best to move carefully.

"You know what I think?" he murmured, a smile curving his lips.

"What do you think?"

"I think you're getting stir-crazy." His smile widened. "I think maybe we could risk getting out of this place for a little while, don't you think?"

She sat up, intrigued. "What do you have in mind?"

"Just go get dressed." He tugged at the quilt. "And bundle up!"

FOR THE FIRST twenty minutes, they seemed to be driving through endless woodland, broken here and there by the striated rock that revealed where the road had been cut through the mountains. Then, as the last of the day's sunlight painted the western sky in hues of amber, rose and purple, the trees thinned out, revealing a picturesque town nestled in a small valley.

"Welcome to Laurel Hollow, Kentucky," Connor said with a smile in his voice. "Population, hmm, somewhere around 250, I think."

"How did you know how to find this place?" she asked, charmed. The town looked like something out of a postcard, a quintessential small Southern town, complete with a tiny white church on the corner with a tall white spire rising into the twilight sky.

"I might have made a call to Quinn while you were napping this afternoon," he said with a smile.

"Just to find a quaint little mountain town to drive through?"

"Not exactly." There was a secret behind his smile, reminding her of the old days, when they were happy and in love. He'd loved to surprise her, something that hadn't always been easy to do, considering her career as an intelligence operative.

He had that same look now.

"What are you up to?" she asked, further intrigued.

His smile grew more mysterious. "You'll see."

Within a couple of miles, the town of Laurel Hollow was a faint glow in the rearview mirror, the scenery replaced by rolling farmland and sporadic lights of houses dotting the landscape here and there. Then they rounded a curve and ahead lay a brightly lit copse of evergreen trees.

Not a copse, she realized as Connor slowed the SUV and turned off the road onto a narrow dirt lane.

It was a tree lot.

"Rebecca Cameron was right," Connor said as he cut the engine and turned to look at her. "No matter what else is going on, we're getting to spend Christmas together this year. And it wasn't very long ago that I didn't think I'd ever get the chance to do that again. So let's do it right."

Tears pricking her eyes, she reached across the

space between them and touched his face. "This is a wonderful surprise."

"Yeah?" He looked so pleased, she thought, struggling against a fresh sting of tears.

Why had she let Dal talk her into walking away from her life? How could she have even contemplated it? If the circumstances had been reversed, she'd have been furious. And deeply, perhaps irrevocably, hurt.

"What are you thinking?" Connor asked, covering her hand with his own, holding her palm in place against his cheek.

"How incredibly unfair I was to you," she admitted.

"You always did undervalue yourself." He released her hand but held her gaze, his eyes sad.

"What can I help y'all with?" The booming voice so close behind her made Risa jump. She turned to find a short, burly man in overalls and a thick fleece-lined denim jacket standing behind them, his weathered face creased with a big smile. "We've got big trees, small trees, fat ones and skinny ones. You just tell ol' Ray what you need and I'll get you just the right tree."

"How about medium-sized?" Connor suggested. "Not too fat, not too thin." He winked at Risa, making her heart turn a little flip.

"That sounds perfect," she agreed with a smile.

"You just head over there to the right side of the lot and you'll find exactly what you want," Ray said, still grinning at them.

Connor reached out and took Risa's hand, giving a light tug. "Let's go find us a Christmas tree."

"WE'VE GOT VISUAL contact with McGinnis." The voice over the phone line was a growly bass, with just a touch of a Boston accent. Adam Lovell was a Harvard washout who had developed an obsequious style early on, perhaps hoping he could make up in sycophancy what he lacked in brainpower.

It hardly made his boss respect the young toady any more, but it did make Adam very, very useful.

"What about the woman?" he asked.

"She's there with him. But she's not wearing a hijab."

Of course she wasn't. She wasn't really a Kaziri widow, after all, no matter how well she'd played the part. She was Georgia born and bred, the daughter of a tough old leatherneck who'd parlayed her mother's Kaziri blood into a career in the CIA.

Damn Martin Dalrymple's wily old hide.

"If you can get your hands on the woman, do it."

"She doesn't seem to be getting very far from Mc-Ginnis."

"So find a way to separate them."

Adam was silent so long he began to wonder if he'd lost the connection to the young man. But finally, Adam spoke, his tone tentative. "May I ask why we're trying to bring this woman into custody?"

"No, you may not," he answered, and ended the call.

He sat back against the buttery leather of his desk chair, staring out the window at the lights of the Na-

tional Mall, blurred by the foggy drizzle that had en-
veloped the capital in a dreary haze. In retrospect,
he should have guessed that Dalrymple would have
had a few tricks up his sleeve. He should have anticipated that Parisa McGinnis might have survived
the explosion. That after years of blending in with
the Kaziri natives in their homeland, she could have
found a way to blend in with the Kaziris who'd fled
to the US.

He had looked for her in North Carolina among
the Christians, thinking she'd have fit in better with
them, given her personal background. But that hadn't
been smart thinking. He was rather embarrassed at
how shortsighted he'd been.

But that was water under the bridge. He'd found
her. She was still alive.

That reality had to be remedied as soon as possible.

"WHAT DO YOU THINK?" Risa asked, cocking her head
as she considered the fir tree that sat in the middle of
the maze of conical-shaped evergreens that filled the
Christmas-tree lot.

Connor seemed to give it some thought, although
she could tell from his expression that he knew this
was the tree for her. Still, he made her wait a few seconds as he stroked his chin and surveyed all sides of
the tree, giving the limbs a few light tugs before he
finally turned his head to look at her.

"I love it," he said.

"Yay!" She wrapped her arms around him and
gave him a hug before she realized she had thrown

away her right to touch him whenever she wanted to. She looked up at him, feeling uncertain and not liking it.

"Remind you of anything?" he asked, smiling as if to put her at ease.

She looked at the tree again, suddenly realizing why she'd liked it on sight. "Our first Christmas tree."

"Yep." Connor touched the fir's thick needles with one finger. "It was almost bigger than your apartment in Germany. Remember?"

She smiled at the image his words conjured in her mind, of a fat little Christmas tree, decked to the hilt with garland and ornaments, taking up half of her tiny economy flat in Günzberg, halfway between her assignment at the US Consulate in Munich and Connor's temporary duty at the Marine Corps' Camp Panzer Kaserne in Böblingen. "I remember."

"Remember that night we had some of the guys at the base over for a party and we could barely move around because of that bloody tree?" He laughed softly.

"And then you proposed after they left. Because you said they all told you if you didn't, one of them would."

His smile broadened, and he looked as if the memory made him genuinely happy. Risa felt her throat tightening, waiting for him to realize the past was truly past and the present was full of lies and regrets.

But before his expression had a chance to change,

the tree lot proprietor, Ray, appeared as if out of the ether. "Found one you like?"

"Yes, sir," Connor said. "We'll take this one."

Ray gave them a price that seemed fair. Connor pulled out his wallet and paid in cash. "Don't suppose you have a wheelbarrow or something I can use to cart it to my truck."

"Of course I do." He flashed Connor a smile of pure delight. "Anything else I can help y'all with tonight?"

"Do you know any place where we can find some reasonably priced decorations?" Risa asked. "Doesn't have to be anything fancy."

"As a matter of fact, you're already in the right place." Ray turned his grin toward her and waved his hand to one side. "Back yonder, you'll find a shed where we have all sorts of genuine handmade ornaments made by some of Kentucky's most gifted local artisans."

Those artisans were probably Ray's wife and kids, Risa thought, but she wasn't in any position to be picky. "Just back that way?"

"Yes, ma'am." Ray turned to help Connor pick up the tree.

"I'll catch up," she told Connor, giving his arm a pat and heading in the direction Ray had indicated.

"Back yonder" was farther away than she'd realized, as she weaved her way through the maze of evergreen trees. Night had fallen completely during the time she and Connor had been selecting their tree, the darkness broken only by a string of bare bulbs hung along a series of garden stakes planted in the soft ground of the tree lot. They were apparently powered by a generator, as she could hear the equipment humming somewhere nearby.

A light wind had begun to pick up, making the lightbulbs sway, casting eerie, dancing shadows across the ground. Risa tugged her coat more tightly around her, trying to ignore the sudden prickle of unease that rippled its way down her spine.

It's just the wind, she reminded herself. She wasn't back in Cincinnati anymore. She was in nowhere, Kentucky, where nobody knew her from Adam or Eve. Connor was just a few short yards away.

She turned around to reassure herself that he was within sight.

But she saw nothing but trees.

For a second, she felt a frisson of panic. But she calmed herself quickly. The road was nearby. All she had to do was follow the string of lights back to where Connor waited with their lovely new tree.

Meanwhile, they had ornaments to select.

She kept heading toward the back of the lot, following the string of lights, until she thought she spotted the edge of a wooden shed peeking through the gaps in the trees. She started to relax.

Then, with shocking suddenness, the lights went out.

As CONNOR FINISHED securing the fir tree in the back of the Tahoe, the night went suddenly dark. Only the dome light inside the truck relieved the bottomless gloom that fell over the tree lot behind him.

"What the hell?" Ray's voice carried through the darkness.

There was a flashlight in the SUV's glove box. Connor retrieved it and turned it on, a strong beam of light slashing through the blackness. It played across Ray's weathered features, making the man squint and hold up his hand against the glare.

Connor moved the light away from Ray's face as he walked closer. "What happened?"

"Not sure," Ray answered, frowning. "The generator's back this way." He waved for Connor to follow him with the flashlight as he turned and entered the tree maze.

Connor followed, not liking the sudden darkness. As a retired marine, he was used to making the dark work for him, but he wasn't equipped to handle the loss of easy visibility, especially when he was separated from Risa. The light outage was probably a coincidence.

But he didn't like coincidences. Especially not now.

"What the hell?" Ray said again, sounding even more confounded than before.

"What?" Connor asked.

Ray held out his hand. "Can I borrow that?"

Reluctantly, Connor handed over the flashlight. Ray played the light across a small open area in the middle of the tree lot. Connor could see what looked like a generator wheel kit, but there was no generator contained within the frame.

"Well, hell," Ray said, sounding annoyed. "Who the hell took my damn generator?"

Connor's heart skipping a beat, he grabbed the flashlight back from Ray and started to play the beam of light across the trees ahead of him. "Risa?" he called.

But Risa didn't answer.

Chapter Ten

Risa's pulse hammered loudly in her ears as she tried to orient herself in the darkness. There was a furtive sounding rustle nearby, as if someone were moving through the densely packed trees in an attempt at stealth.

Or was she just imagining things? There was any number of reasons the lights of the tree lot could have gone out, starting with a generator failure.

"Risa!" Connor's voice carried across the tree lot.

And the furtive rustling stopped.

Someone was definitely out there. And if she responded to Connor's call, that someone would know exactly where she was.

She eased backward, wincing when she bumped into one of the trees, setting its limbs rattling softly against one another. She heard the sound of movement again, coming her way.

"Risa?" Connor's voice was closer now, and she realized she was seeing flashes of light moving toward her through the trees. A flashlight?

She remained quiet, letting Connor do all the moving. He was getting closer, although he was a few rows of trees away from where she was crouched.

Suddenly, the sound of movement in the trees nearby picked up, moving away from the light.

She risked edging closer to where Connor was weaving his way through the trees, calling his name when, finally, she could see him only a few feet away. "Connor!"

He pushed through the trees, sending a couple of them toppling, stands and all, to reach her. "Why didn't you answer?" he asked breathlessly, wrapping one strong arm around her waist and pulling her to him.

"There's someone out there," she whispered. "I think they might have been following me."

His only answer was to take her hand and lead her back to the roadside, where the SUV was still parked, a big black shadow in the unrelenting gloom. In a rustle of tree limbs, Ray emerged as well, stepping into the small circle of light cast by Connor's flashlight beam.

"I found the generator," he told Connor. "Someone had dragged it a few dozen yards away and emptied out all the gas."

Connor slanted a look at Risa. "Must have been some kids, pulling a stupid prank."

Ray's lips curved in a grimace of a smile. "Or some of my competitors, out to screw up my night's worth of sales."

Connor rubbed Risa's back, his touch warm and comforting. "You have a lot of trouble with your competitors?"

"Christmas is a cutthroat business."

"What are you going to do now?" Risa asked, trying to settle her jangling nerves. It was possible Ray was right, that one of his competitors had tried to sabotage his business.

Possible. But not likely.

Ray pulled out his phone. "I'll call my wife to bring me some more gas. Get the lights up and running again, and then the kids and me can clean up that mess where those jerks poured out the gas." He nodded at their truck. "Go on, I'll be fine. Maybe y'all can come back out tomorrow when it's light and buy your decorations. I'll give you half price on 'em for your trouble."

Risa looked up at Connor, not sure she wanted to leave Ray alone, under the circumstances. He read her expression and gave a slight nod before he turned to Ray. "Actually, if it's no problem, we'll wait here with you. I'd like to go ahead and get the decorations tonight."

"If you're sure?"

"Positive," Risa agreed.

Ray flashed them a quick grin. "Mighty friendly of you." He pulled his cell phone from the pocket of his jacket and walked a few yards away to make his call.

"I don't think it was his competition," Connor murmured, his lips so close to her ear she felt his breath stir her hair.

"I don't, either."

"Whoever it was, I don't think he went far. He's probably out there somewhere, waiting for a chance to follow us wherever we go next."

"Which can't be back to the safe house," Risa murmured. "At least, not tonight. Agreed?"

"Agreed."

"Who do we think it is?"

"I think the more pressing question is, how did they find us?"

Down the road, headlights appeared in the gloom. Seconds later, Risa heard the rumble of a vehicle engine. Instinctively, she edged closer to Connor, who tucked her under his arm and turned so that his body was between her and the advancing vehicle.

"It's Carla." Ray moved past them toward the roadside as the vehicle, an older-model Chevrolet truck, slowed to a stop.

A short, plump woman with faded red hair and a round, pretty face stepped out of the driver's seat and glanced at Risa and Connor before she turned to look at her husband, who had retrieved a plastic gas container from the bed of the pickup. "What happened?" she asked as she handed him the flashlight she held in her right hand.

"Must've been a kid pulling a prank," Ray told her. "Thanks for gettin' here so quick, hon."

Carla slanted another curious look at Risa and Connor.

Ray nodded in their direction. "Sorry, didn't get your names."

"Mac and Marisa," Connor said before Risa could speak. "Nice to meet you. We were about to look at some decorations out back when the lights went out."

"Well, I can help you out with that," Carla said

with a smile as Ray turned on the flashlight and headed into the maze of trees. "I brought a couple more boxes of ornaments and garlands the girls put together—the local girls' clubs in town make money for their activities by doing arts and crafts. Both of our girls are involved, so we sell 'em here at the tree lot every Christmas. Want to take a look and see if there's anything you like?" She reached into the back of the truck, hauled out a large cardboard box and set it on the ground by the truck.

Risa glanced at Connor, wondering if they dared stay there any longer. It wasn't like she could be sure they'd get a chance to use that tree they'd just bought, not if they were about to go on the run. Plus, money was about to become a real problem for them.

"We'll take a look," Connor said, meeting her gaze with steel in his blue eyes. He pointed the beam of his flashlight toward the box.

Carla opened the box to reveal several small ornaments, individually sealed in clear plastic zip-top bags. Some had been carved from wood and painted, the quality surprisingly sophisticated. Others were made of needlework or handwoven, in homey colors that reminded Risa of some of the craft work she'd seen in the small villages of Kaziristan when she'd been living there undercover.

"They're beautiful," she said.

"Thank you. I'll be sure to pass along the compliments to the girls. Anything you like? They're fifty cents an ornament, and the beaded and woven garland strands are two dollars apiece."

Risa selected three wood-beaded garlands, two frosty blue and the other a weathered gold. She also selected a couple dozen ornaments in complementary colors. Connor pulled fifteen dollars from his wallet and handed it over just as the generator roared to life somewhere in the middle of the tree lot. The string of bulbs flickered on, lighting up the darkness.

"Thank you for everything," Connor told Ray when he emerged from the thicket. "Hope you have a merry Christmas!"

"Enjoy your tree and decorations!" Ray gave a wave as they packed their decorations in the back of the truck with the tree. Risa waved back as they drove away from the brightness of the tree lot.

Ahead, the winding road seemed to disappear into inky blackness beyond the beams of the truck's headlights. Risa quelled a shiver and turned to look at Connor. "How the hell did someone find us?"

IN CUMBERLAND, CONNOR found what he was looking for—a public establishment still open at 8:00 p.m., with enough cars in the parking lot that an open ambush would be hard to accomplish. In this case, it was a pizza restaurant with a parking lot almost full on this cold Friday night.

"You're hungry?" Risa asked, her tone dry, as Connor pulled into the parking lot and angled the truck into a place near the back.

"It's dinnertime," he murmured as he cut the engine.

"Seriously, what are we doing here?"

"Getting dinner," he answered, lifting one finger to his lips.

Risa's eyes narrowed, but she understood the unspoken order.

Connor reached into the glove compartment and pulled out a small rectangular box. Inside was an RF detector, designed to pick up signals from wireless transmitters, such as listening devices. He switched it on and waited for it to scan for a signal. It detected a GPS signal—Quinn put GPS trackers on all of the company's fleet vehicles—but nothing else.

"No bugs," he told her. "You can speak freely."

"What's that picking up?" she asked, pointing to the flashing green light.

"GPS—this is a company vehicle, so they'll be tracking it."

"What if someone at Campbell Cove Security is the one who's following us? Maybe they needed to make covert contact."

Connor shook his head. "Someone would have found a way to let me know he or she was there. No reason to disable the generator and make such a production."

"So nobody's bugging the car, or us. How did they find us? We need to figure that out, because they may be following us right now."

"I don't know," he admitted. "I know we weren't directly followed this time—as dark as it was on the road driving here, nobody could've followed without my knowing it."

"Does that make any sense?" Risa tugged her coat

more tightly around her, looking spooked. "They risked following me around that tree lot with you and Ray there, but they don't even try to follow us when we leave the place?"

She was right. It didn't make any sense. Unless—

"Damn it," he growled, snapping open the driver's door. He grabbed the flashlight from the console compartment and started examining the underside of the Tahoe.

Risa came around the truck to stand beside him. "You said the RF detector picked up the GPS signal. What if—"

"Exactly." He spotted the tracker that Campbell Cove Security placed on all the fleet vehicles, as expected.

But a few inches farther down the underside of the chassis, he found another small tracker, almost invisible against the mud-spattered undercarriage. He checked to make sure it wasn't connected to anything that could damage the car if he removed it, then plucked it from the undercarriage.

"If we could put it on another vehicle..." Risa looked up at him, her eyes dark and unreadable.

"We'd be putting the driver of that vehicle in danger."

She nodded. "I guess we can just throw it away."

He looked around the parking lot, trying to come up with an option besides leaving it sitting, static, in the parking lot of the pizza restaurant. It wasn't a terrible option, he supposed, but for their purposes, it would help if the tracker could be on the move for a while, maybe drawing the people following them on a wild goose chase.

"The river," Risa said.

He looked at her. "The river?"

"We crossed a river on the way here," Risa said. "We could throw it in the river."

"The electronics would short out. It wouldn't give us any lead time."

She grinned at him, and for a second, he felt transported back to the early days of their relationship, when just being together was enough to make them both feel giddy and light. "Luckily for us, we just bought a whole lot of plastic-wrapped ornaments from the crafty girls of eastern Kentucky."

"Brilliant," he said, opening the back of the Tahoe to retrieve one of the bags. "Which way is the river?

"SOMETHING ISN'T RIGHT." Risa stared out the windshield at the darkness, unease rising in her chest. They'd dumped the GPS tracker in the Poor Fork tributary fifteen minutes ago and gotten rid of the Campbell Cove Security tracker as well. Now they were driving west toward Harlan, but she didn't feel any safer. "How did they connect the Tahoe to me? I don't have any relationship to Campbell Cove Security. And this is a fleet vehicle."

"You have a relationship to me," Connor said grimly. "And I was using my real name and my real credit cards in Cincinnati."

"But that only works if…"

"If they made you." Connor glanced at her. In the

light from the dashboard, his face was a road map of shadows, but she could see enough of his expression to know it was grim.

"That has to be it. They made me. And they connected me to you."

"So they're tracking me, not you."

"Not anymore," she said. "We don't use your credit cards anymore. Throw away your phone if it can be connected to you."

"I have a burner phone that should be safe."

"Stick with that. How much cash do you have?"

"About a thousand in a lockbox under your seat. Another five hundred back at the safe house."

"We can't go back there."

"No," he agreed. "Do you have any cash?"

"Three hundred in a hidden pocket in my backpack."

"Also back at the safe house?"

"Actually, no. I stashed my backpack under the backseat before we left. After the close call in Cincinnati, I didn't think it was a good idea to let my laptop get too far out of my sight."

"We can't use your phone to connect to the web."

"No, but maybe we can spare a couple hundred dollars to buy a new burner we can use instead," she said, her sense of equilibrium beginning to return. "Also, I don't think we can risk getting in touch with Campbell Cove Security. At least not for a few days, until we can figure out if they've linked you directly to the company. It's possible they put the tracker on the Tahoe after we left Cincinnati, maybe at that gas station where we stopped outside Lexington."

"Quinn will start looking for us if we don't check in. And if he sends someone to the safe house to check on us and finds us missing—"

"I know," she interrupted, "but it's a risk we have to take. At least until we get some distance from where our last tracking coordinates show up. Let's just look for a low-rent motel that'll take cash and ask no questions. Get a good night's sleep and then we can worry about what comes tomorrow."

Connor was silent for a long moment, long enough that she was beginning to fear he was going to argue. But finally, he nodded. "Okay. You're right. We're cold, we're exhausted, and I don't know about you, but I'm starving. Maybe we can find a late-night drive-through on the way."

Her stomach rumbled in response, making them both laugh. She rubbed her stomach, where the baby was kicking up a storm. "Junior votes yes to the food, too."

Connor reached across the space between them, resting his hand on hers where it lay on her stomach. "We never talked about kids before."

"We hadn't been married that long." She took his hand and pressed it against her belly. "We thought we had time."

Connor's fingers flexed against her stomach. "Time. Everybody think there's time. Until there's not."

The baby kicked against her belly, and she heard Connor's soft gasp of surprise. She suppressed a smile. "And sometimes, you just have to figure out how to make more time for what's important."

"Like Junior."

Exactly, she thought, blinking back the sting of tears.

THE REST STOP Motor Lodge a few miles west of Harlan was two stories of shabby brick and mortar, held together, the best Connor could tell, primarily by years' worth of grime. The bedding on the double bed in the room they rented for the night looked relatively clean, but just in case, Connor retrieved the emergency camping kit from the SUV and spread the two sleeping bags over the bedding for them.

"Resourceful," Risa said, her tone approving as she sat down on one side of the bed, her legs crossed beneath her rounded belly. Digging in the bags they'd picked up at a burger joint on the way out of Cumberland, she retrieved a small box of French fries and started nibbling.

She grinned at him as she passed him the bag, feeling a strange sort of exhilaration as the food hit her empty stomach. Or maybe it was just the feeling that she was, finally, herself again, after months of being someone else. She was Risa McGinnis, she was with the man she loved, and she was weeks away from giving birth to their child.

Even the threat of ever-present danger didn't seem to quell her sense that she was finally where she was supposed to be.

But the sight of Connor's sober face took a little

edge off her sudden sense of well-being. He ate his hamburger slowly, methodically, as if his mind was somewhere far away.

Back at Campbell Cove Security? Or somewhere else altogether?

Something Dal had told her a couple of weeks ago, when she'd asked if he knew anything about what Connor was doing now, flashed through her mind, chilling her mood further.

Seven months is a long time when you think your wife is dead.

Chapter Eleven

The Friday night crowd at The Jewel of Tablis was larger than Maddox Heller had anticipated. For cover, he'd brought along his wife, Iris, for this trip, leaving their two children with Iris's sister Rose and her husband, Daniel, who'd been nearby in Lexington for the week doing research for Daniel's latest book on criminal profiling. They'd agreed to take the kids through the weekend.

"That's Farid," he murmured to Iris, glancing toward the emailed photo saved on his phone. "Quinn and Cameron said he might be the weak link. If we can convince him it's worth his while to tell us why the man wanted to look around inside Risa's apartment."

"Do you think it was really Tahir Mahmoud?" Iris was trying to appear unfazed, but he knew the thought that Mahmoud might still be alive disturbed her. The man had nearly killed her eight years ago. She'd had nightmares about him for a couple of years before she'd finally managed to conquer the residual fears of that encounter.

"You saw the photo," he said, wishing he could give her a definitive no. But he and Iris didn't lie to each other. It was one of the cardinal rules of their marriage.

"I did."

"What did *you* think?"

"It looked a lot like him," she said after a brief pause. "Damn Alexander Quinn for telling you they'd found the body when they hadn't."

He reached across the table and took her hand. As always, he felt a light quiver of energy where their fingers touched. "Are you afraid he'll come after us?"

"I don't know." Her fingers tightened under his. "I guess it's a plus that he hasn't bothered us in eight years. Assuming he's still alive."

"That's how I'm choosing to look at it," he admitted. "But I've asked Quinn to harden the security at our new house, just in case."

"What about the kids? Daisy rides a bus to a public school every day. Jacob is about to start school next year. How do we protect them?"

"By finding out if this guy really is Tahir Mahmoud," Maddox said quietly, glancing across the restaurant at a pretty young woman wearing a bright green scarf over her lustrous dark hair. Darya Nahir. Risa McGinnis had identified the young waitress as a person to interview, since she had waited on the table of the men in question and might have gleaned a little information about them. "There's Darya. You ready?"

Iris nodded. "Showtime."

Darya approached their table, a friendly smile on

her face and a pair of menus in her hands. "Welcome to The Jewel of Tablis. Would you like something to drink while you're looking at your menus?"

"I'll take a mint tea, iced," Maddox said. "Sweetheart?"

"The same, only I want mine hot." Iris smiled up at Darya. "That is a gorgeous *roosari*. It looks handmade."

Darya smiled. "It was. My mother made it."

"The embroidery work is exquisite."

"Thank you." Darya looked pleased by the compliment.

"Oh, I bet you're the girl Con was telling us about."

Darya's dark eyebrows lifted as she finished jotting down their drink orders. "Con?"

"Connor. A friend of ours who was in town earlier this week. He's the one who recommended the restaurant to us. I think he was here the other night—maybe Tuesday or Wednesday? He couldn't stop talking about the pretty waitress he saw—he said she was beautiful, like a bright flower."

"Wow, I don't know if he was talking about me."

"Well, you're definitely not the other waitress he mentioned," Iris said with a laugh. "That woman was about nine months pregnant."

"Yasmin," Darya said, her smile fading. "Yes."

"Is something wrong?" Iris put her hand on the young woman's arm. Her fingers trembled, and Darya gave her a curious look.

"I'm a little worried," Darya admitted. "Yasmin

was supposed to work the past two nights but she didn't show, and she's not answering her phone."

"Do you think she had her baby?" Iris asked, dropping her hand away from the young waitress's arm. She slanted a look at Maddox, her light brown eyes dark with meaning.

Darya gave Iris a troubled look. "I don't know. Farid—our boss—tells me not to worry, but it hasn't really made me feel any better. I wish I knew what happened to her." She cleared her expression deliberately, flashing them a smile that wasn't quite convincing. "I'll be back in a few minutes for your order."

Maddox waited until Darya was out of earshot before he leaned across the table toward his wife. "Well?"

"She's tense. Definitely worried about Risa. If there's a terrorist plot cooking in this town, she's not part of it."

"Then maybe she could be an ally," he murmured.

"Maybe," Iris agreed. "But I think the person who can really tell us the most about what happened here Wednesday night is her boss."

Maddox glanced across the room, where Farid Rahimi stood talking to a couple sitting at a table in the corner. From this angle, he looked vaguely familiar.

Where had he seen him before?

As WEARY AS he was, after the past two eventful days, Connor found that sleep was elusive. Beside him, Risa had fallen into an occasionally restless slumber, lying on her side, her body curled up around her pregnant belly as if she were protecting her child, even in slumber.

He lay on his back, gazing up at the ceiling, where the faint thread of light seeping in through the motel room curtains cast odd shadows on the water-stained Sheetrock.

Something wasn't right. Actually, a lot wasn't right, but the one thing that continued to bug him was how quickly their pursuers had found them at the Christmas-tree lot.

They'd guessed that the tracker might have been added to the car when they stopped in Lexington. But how had anyone found them in Lexington if they didn't already know where to look for them? He was pretty sure he hadn't been followed out of town, at least once they hit the long stretch of highway between Cincinnati and Lexington. So either someone had spotted them leaving together in Cincinnati, seen the direction they were going and made a calculated guess about their route, or…

That's where he hit a wall. What was the "or"? Was there any other way someone could have put a tracker on the car before they arrived at the safe house?

"You're still awake, aren't you?" Risa's sleepy voice rasped softly in the dark.

"How did someone put a tracker on the Tahoe?"

She rolled over, propping her head on her hand and looking at him. "You said you thought it was when we stopped in Lexington."

"But how did someone find us in Lexington that fast? Yes, I know I used my credit card, but we were gone within a few minutes after that transaction was processed. No way did anyone have time to reach our location and put the GPS tracker on the Tahoe that quickly."

"You're right," she said, her voice sober. "So someone was either expecting us to be in Lexington, at that place we stopped, or..."

"Or someone had already put the tracker on the Tahoe in Cincinnati."

"But it's Quinn's car."

"I know." He rolled over to face her, a light shiver running down his spine as he studied her features in the dim light. She was so familiar to him, and yet, somehow after these seven months apart, she seemed like a stranger. A beautiful, intoxicating, very pregnant stranger.

"Maybe someone was tracking Quinn."

Possible, he supposed, though his new boss was known for his fanatical security measures. "I don't think they would have been able to put the tracker on the Tahoe until Cincinnati," he murmured. "Quinn would have had the vehicle checked before he left Campbell Cove. But someone could have spotted him when he arrived and put the tracker on his vehicle then."

"So maybe it's really someone after Quinn?" she asked hopefully.

"Maybe." But he didn't think so. Whoever had disabled the generator at the tree lot had to have known that Connor and Risa were the people in the SUV. He growled. "I can't make this make sense. Even

well-organized terrorist groups don't have the resources to be so Johnny-on-the-spot with surveillance. Do they?"

"No," she agreed. "They're more and more techno-
logically savvy these days, yes, but what you're suggesting would have to be…" She frowned, shadows
falling over her eyes as her brow furrowed.

"It would have to be a government," he finished
for her. "And Kaziristan sure as hell doesn't have that
sort of capability."

"No. But people in our own country do," she said
soberly.

"You think our own government could be behind
this?" It seemed to physically hurt to say those words
aloud. He'd dedicated the better part of his adult life
to serving the government of the United States. And
while he certainly didn't trust every member of the
bureaucratic behemoth that was the federal government, he couldn't believe his country would target a
woman who had given most of her own adult life in
government service.

"I don't know," she said. "I don't want to believe
it, but it wouldn't exactly be the first time someone
in government went rogue, would it? Barton Reid's
treason wasn't that long ago, after all. Ask Maddox
Heller."

Barton Reid had been a State Department official
who'd played terrorists and other enemy elements
against the US government for his own financial
gain. A lot of damage had been done before the man

was taken down and sentenced to life in prison for his treachery.

Could the attempt on Risa's life have been ordered by another government official gone rogue?

"But why would you have been targeted?" he asked. "What were you working on last? Is it something you can tell me about?"

"The last thing I was working on was pretty mundane. And kind of gross." She rolled over onto her back, gazing up at the ceiling, a smile playing at her lips. "I was tasked with doing basic background analysis and surveillance on a group of Kaziri entrepreneurs who were planning to start an agri-tech company. Their goal was to research and implement the best agricultural practices for Kaziristan's climate and ecosystem. You know, selecting drought-resistant crops and livestock that have the best chance of thriving in Kaziristan. They were looking for UN grants as well as grants from the US and the government of Kaziristan."

"That sounds...fun." Connor's tone sounded skeptical.

"Actually, they were nice guys. Young, forward-thinking. Well-educated and hoping to pull even the rural parts of Kaziristan kicking and screaming into the twenty-first century. They wanted to improve the chances of profitable agriculture in Kaziristan that didn't include growing poppies for warlords to turn into drugs to fund their turf battles."

"Did you turn in your final report before the crash?"

"If things had gone smoothly, I would have been able to give them a green light, but something came up at the last minute that was going to require more investigation. I was supposed to meet with another agent when I got back to DC, but…"

"But you didn't get there." He nodded. "So, what was the holdup?"

"One of the big things the guys wanted to do was harvest bat guano from the caves in the mountains. From a chemistry standpoint, it was showing great promise as an affordable, effective fertilizer for some of the crops that needed extra nutrients not available in the soil. But the guys discovered that some of the bats in the area they were targeting had started coming down with a hemorrhagic disease. At the time of my investigation, the disease hadn't jumped into another species as far as we could tell, but there was a very strong concern that the disease might spread to livestock or even humans through the guano."

"That doesn't seem as if it should have put a stop to the project," Connor said. "It was just one source of fertilizer, right?"

"Yes, but it was a pretty significant part of the cost-control aspect of their plan. Other sources of fertilizer, like cow and goat manure, weren't naturally occurring the way the bat guano was."

"That's what you were coming back to DC to discuss?"

"Yes. I was supposed to meet with someone in the CDC to determine if there was a way to test the guano on-site to ascertain whether the bats in the area were diseased, and what kind of costs that might incur. Also, I was hoping to meet with some people in the Department of Agriculture to see what protocols for food safety might be involved."

"And they say a career in the CIA is mostly a big bore."

She smiled. "I know it sounds kind of dull, but if these guys were able to accomplish their goals, it could mean that hundreds of thousands of people in rural Kaziristan could live vastly improved lives."

"Well, it certainly doesn't sound like anything that would put you on a hit list," Connor agreed. "But I guess it's something we should look into."

"How do you propose we do that? How do we look into anything at this point?" Her voice was tight with frustration. "Do we dare risk trying to contact Quinn if someone's out there tracking your electronic trail?"

"I have enough cash to buy a burner phone. Nobody will know to track it, and we can reach Quinn that way."

"Unless they're tracking Quinn's electronic trail, too."

"Quinn is pretty savvy. It would be hard to track him without his knowing it."

"It's still a risk," she warned. "But since we don't have internet access at the moment, he may be our only option to do a little digging into that possibility."

He turned over, facing her. "We can't do anything before morning. So why don't you try to stop those wheels in your head from turning and get some sleep?"

Her lips twitched up at the corners.

"What?" he asked.

"Remember how you used to help me go to sleep when my mind wouldn't stop running in circles?"

He did. Vividly. "I could give it a try."

Her eyes widened. "You're serious?"

"Turn over."

She stared at him, her dark eyes gleaming in the low light. Then she rolled over to her other side and went very still.

He shifted until her body was spooned against his. She felt small and deliciously warm, tucked against him beneath the blankets. He could feel the tension in her body, as tangible as a low-level electric current running through her muscles.

Starting with her neck, he pressed his thumb against the taut muscles, rubbing firmly but gently, trying to work loose some of the tension. Moving relentlessly downward, he followed the curve of her arm, down to her hand, where he massaged each finger. Then he traced the curve of her hip, gently massaging the muscles of her outer thigh.

"Helping?" he murmured, struggling to hold his own body in check.

"Mmm," she answered with a guttural groan of pleasure.

So not what he needed.

His fingers trembled as he sat up and worked his way down her calves, kneading the knotted muscles.

"Don't," she whispered as he reached her ankle. She turned onto her back and sat up, turning to look at him. She was breathing hard, her chest rising and falling beneath her thin T-shirt. "You forgot how these moments always ended."

He curled his hand behind the back of her head, tangling his fingers in her hair. He tugged her closer, whispering against her lips. "I didn't forget."

Her lips parted, her breath hot on his mouth as he kissed her.

He'd kissed her hundreds, thousands of times before, but this felt strangely new somehow, as if it was the first time. She darted her tongue lightly across his lower lip, tasting. Testing.

He ran his hands down her sides, letting them settle lightly over the bulge of her belly. He kissed her again, more deeply. With more intensity. Reacquainting himself with the taste of her, with the sweet headiness of her scent. She responded with eagerness, curling her fingers in his hair as she rose to her knees and took control of the kiss with a fierce passion that made his head spin.

"I missed you. Every day." She kissed her way across his jaw and down the side of his neck, nipping lightly at his skin. "Every night."

He was losing all control. Had this been what he'd been hoping for when he offered to help her get to sleep?

She lowered herself until she was straddling his hips, the heat of her body enveloping his. Claiming him all over again.

Branding him with her need.

He had lost all restraint now, his body surging

with desire as she pressed herself harder against his erection.

"It's okay," she whispered against his throat. "This doesn't have to mean anything beyond this moment."

Her words worked like an ice bath, cooling his runaway ardor. He found the strength to pull away from her grasp, to put distance between them on the bed until he was able to recapture his breath.

"I'm not ready for this," he admitted. "I can't just pretend it doesn't mean anything. I can't act as if everything between us is okay now."

She sank back against the pillows, her breaths coming fast and harsh. "I know." Her hands moved to her belly, stroking, soothing, as she struggled to get her breathing back under control.

"I'm not saying never," he added, even though a part of him wished he could. The raw, vulnerable part that wanted to pretend that if he didn't let her back in his heart, he'd never be hurt again. But he knew better now. There was no escaping what he felt for her.

He was just going to have to find some way to deal with it.

"I understand," she murmured, her hands playing over her round belly.

He rolled over on his side, his back to her. Needing what little space, what little distance, he could put between them in this tiny motel room.

FARID RAHIMI LEFT his apartment building around seven the next morning, dressed in sweats and a thick fleece jacket. The North Face, Maddox noticed.

High end, top quality. The restaurant business must be doing well for him. Or he had another source of income.

He couldn't shake the sense that he'd seen the man before. But it hadn't been in Kaziristan, when Maddox was working as a Marine Security Guard at the US Embassy in Tablis.

It was somewhere else, more recently.

"Still can't remember where you know him from?" Iris sat beside him in the passenger seat of the truck, wrapped up against the cold and sipping a hot coffee.

"No. It's not from my time in Kaziristan, I'm pretty sure."

"Any word on the background check?"

Maddox gave himself a mental kick and checked his phone. There was a new email from Kyra Sanchez at the office. The subject line read Background.

He opened the email and scanned the contents. "Hmm."

"Hmm?"

"Rahimi held a job in Mariposa at the American Consulate for a couple of years."

"Maybe that's where you know him from?"

"Maybe." He started the truck and began following Rahimi, who was now jogging up the street toward Washington Park. He found a place to park the truck on the street and kept an eye on Rahimi as the man started running a brisk circuit of the park.

"Interesting that a Kaziri man ends up working in the US Consulate on a tiny Caribbean island," Iris murmured. "And Quinn worked there, too, didn't he?"

Maddox dragged his gaze away from Rahimi long enough to look at his wife. "What are you thinking?"

She took another sip of coffee, her dark eyes meeting his over the rim of the cup. "Wouldn't be the first time Alexander Quinn was running an op without telling you about it."

He looked back at Rahimi, taking in the trim physique and strong running form. Not the kind of fitness he'd normally associate with your average middle-aged restaurateur.

He picked up his phone and dialed a number. Quinn answered on the first ring. "Quinn."

"Heller," he snapped back. "When were you going to tell me that Farid Rahimi is on our payroll?"

"Need to know, Heller." Quinn's voice tightened. "We've got a bigger problem. The McGinnises have dumped the tracker on the Tahoe. They've gone rogue."

Chapter Twelve

"I've been thinking about the Tahoe," Risa said over their breakfast of cheese crackers and sodas from the vending machines next to the motel office.

"You think we need to ditch it somewhere."

She nodded. "If there's any possibility we're being tracked by someone with access to government resources, we need to take measures to thwart them."

"You're right. We're lucky they haven't tracked us already."

"If we'd stayed in a normal motel room, management might well have asked for our license plate number when we registered." Risa finished the last of her crackers and downed the rest of the Sprite he'd bought.

"That's why I went for a place where nobody would ask any questions."

"Do you think Quinn has figured out we're not at the safe house yet?"

"Probably," Connor conceded. "Someone will have noticed that the GPS tracker was disabled. We didn't put it in a plastic bag the way we did with the rogue tracker. The next step is to check the safe house."

"So they must know we've gone."

He nodded. "If we ditch the Tahoe, how are we going to get around? I don't want to steal a car, and we don't have enough money to buy one, even a piece-of-garbage car."

She bit her lip, thinking. She wasn't nearly as certain as Connor that Alexander Quinn was playing things straight with them, but Connor was right about one thing—if they wanted to have the mobility to stay on the run, they needed transportation. And she wasn't any more inclined to grand theft auto than he was.

"Who do you trust the most at Campbell Cove Security?" she asked him.

"Heller," he answered immediately.

"Any way to get in touch with him without anyone else at Spear knowing about it?"

He gave it a moment's thought before he smiled. "As a matter of fact, yes."

TEN MINUTES LATER, they stood outside a small gas station on the main road, huddling together against the frigid cold and praying that the pay phone hanging on the front of the attached food mart was in service.

Connor breathed a sigh of relief at the dial tone. He punched in the number jotted in his address book and waited for a response. "Please answer," he muttered.

Next to him, Risa edged closer, as if seeking his

warmth. He put his arm around her shoulders, tugging her closer.

On the fourth ring, as he was starting to lose hope, a woman's voice replied, "Hello?"

"Iris, it's Connor McGinnis. I need to talk to Maddox. Is he with you?"

A moment later, Maddox's gravelly drawl answered. "Where the hell are you, Connor?"

"We had to run. Someone put a tracker on the SUV—besides the Campbell Cove Security tracker. Whoever it was tried to get his hands on Risa last night at a place we stopped. We didn't think it was smart to return to the safe house."

"Good call," Maddox said. "Why'd you call Iris's number?"

"We don't know who might be trying to find us or how they're doing it. I didn't think it would be wise to call a company-connected phone, but I hoped I might catch you with Iris."

"You lucked out. What do you need?"

Connor glanced at Risa. They had discussed what they'd ask for on the way to find a pay phone, but now that it was time to make their demands, he was beginning to wonder if they weren't being a little too paranoid.

"Connor?" Maddox asked.

"I'm here," he said, looking at Risa. He covered the mouthpiece of the phone. "Are you sure this is how you want to do it?"

She nodded.

"We need a car that can't be connected to Campbell Cove Security. And I don't want Quinn to know I contacted you. Can you do that?"

Maddox was quiet for a moment. "Yeah. I can do that. But I want to see you. I need to talk to you face-to-face. Do you trust me to do that?"

"He wants to meet with us," Connor told Risa.

Her brow furrowed, but after a moment, she nodded. "Tell him not to use a vehicle that could be easily connected to him."

Connor relayed the request.

"I'll make it happen," Maddox agreed. "Where and when?"

Connor thought fast. "You know that sandwich shop next to the dollar store in Cumberland? Think you can get there by lunchtime?"

"It'll be cutting it close, but yeah. I should be able to."

"See you at twelve thirty." Connor hung up the phone and looked at Risa. "We're set."

She looked tense. "You think I'm paranoid."

"Maybe a little. But we have to keep you and the munchkin safe, don't we?"

She rubbed her stomach. "So what do we do while we're waiting?"

"There's a public library in Cumberland. Why don't we see if we can find a free internet connection?"

THE PUBLIC LIBRARY was doing a brisk business that Saturday morning, mostly parents with young children who were there for a special reading of Clement

Moore's famous poem, "A Visit from St. Nicholas." They passed the group of rapt children listening to the tale of the night before Christmas on their way to the computer terminals.

"We'll be reading that poem to Junior next Christmas," Connor murmured.

Risa slanted a glance at him, noting the faint look of amazement in his blue eyes and wondering if he realized he'd used the word *we*. Deciding not to push, she followed him to the computer area, where they found that three of the terminals were open. He went to the one that was the farthest away from other library patrons and pulled up a second chair for Risa.

"Okay, what should we look for first?" he asked.

"I can't stop thinking about the project I was supposed to report on before the plane crash, ever since we discussed it last night." She pulled up a search engine and typed in the name of the upstart company.

The first hit came as a shock. "Agri-Tech Entrepreneurs Killed in IED Attack."

"Oh. That's not good," Connor murmured.

She clicked the link, which took her to an English-language paper from Qatar, which reported the death of the two Kaziri businessmen, the owners of the agricultural start-up called Akwat, which loosely translated to "sustenance" in Kaziri. The date of the article was the day after the plane crash.

"Why didn't Dal tell me about this?" Risa wondered.

"I don't know. Maybe he didn't think there was a connection?"

"The day after the plane crash? Isn't that a bit too much of a coincidence?"

Connor frowned. "Maybe not."

She searched deeper in the article for more details. The attack had actually happened the same day as the plane crash, a few hours after the first report of the crash. "It's almost like they waited to be sure I was dead before they struck the agri-tech business."

"But why? Why try to kill all of you?"

"I don't know!" Her voice rose higher than she intended, and a nearby patron gave her a disapproving look. She quickly lowered her voice. "I think we need to get out of here, in case somebody is tracking web searches about Akwat."

"You really think that's possible?"

"It's absolutely possible, if someone has access to national-security internet resources."

Connor lowered his voice to a whisper. "You're talking about someone inside our own government."

"Or China's or Russia's or any number of countries in Europe." She glanced around her, making sure nobody was watching them. "Or hackers, for that matter, if someone was paying them for the information."

"But why? Why would anyone care about an agri-tech start-up business in Kaziristan?"

"Why did anyone want me dead? I don't know. But I need to find out." She rose from her chair and started to reach for the straps of her backpack. Connor beat her to it, swinging the heavy pack over his shoulder.

They made their way back through the library, trying to blend in with the rest of the patrons. They emerged into bright sunlight and a hint of warmth that took the edge off the cold breeze flapping the American flag hanging on a pole outside the library. It was already noon, close to the time they were supposed to meet Maddox Heller at the sandwich shop.

Inside the Tahoe, Connor turned to look at her, his gaze intense. "Whatever this is you're up against, I'm in it with you. You know that, don't you? What I said to you last night—it doesn't change that fact. We're going to figure this out together. We're going to get your life back for you."

She held his gaze, afraid to read too much into what he was saying, especially since he'd said *your life* instead of *our life*. But she found his words heartening anyway. "Okay."

"And then we'll have the time and space to figure out what happens next." He softened his words by reaching out to touch her face, his callused fingers deliciously rough against her cheek.

She closed her fingers over his. *I know what I want already*, she thought, intensely aware of the quivering sensation of the child wriggling in her womb. *I want us to be a family.*

By habit, Connor sat with his back to the wall, facing the door of the sandwich shop, acutely aware of the store's glass-front facade. It wasn't the most secure of meeting places to have chosen, but at least nobody else in the shop seemed to think there was anything amiss about the man and pregnant woman sitting alone at a table for four. They had gone through the buffet line to select their sandwiches—beef and Swiss with tomatoes and peppers for Connor, and chicken salad with spinach and tomatoes for Risa. They had barely unwrapped their sandwiches before Maddox Heller and his wife, Iris, entered the sandwich shop.

Maddox spotted them and gave a wave before he and Iris went through the line for their own sandwiches. Carrying their trays, they joined Connor and Risa at the table.

"Did you know there's a tree in the back of the Tahoe?" Maddox sat across from Connor with a grin that carved deep dimples in his lean cheeks. He'd been a favorite with the female embassy employees during his time with the Marine Security Guards, and he'd not been afraid to take advantage of that popularity during his off hours.

But Maddox was clearly smitten with his pretty brunette wife, Iris, a slim woman with eyes the color of pecan hulls, an odd hue somewhere between brown and gray.

She smiled across the table at Connor before turning her attention to Risa. "Welcome back from the dead."

"Thank you." Risa managed a smile in return before turning her attention to Maddox and his opening statement. "Yes, we're aware we have a tree in the SUV. It's Christmas."

Connor quickly caught them up on the details of what had happened to them the night before. "We don't think we're safe in the Tahoe. They have our tag number and the make and model of the vehicle."

"Yeah, I can see how you'd be worried." Maddox leaned closer across the table, lowering his voice. "We drove here in a Dodge Durango. Rented by my brother-in-law, and there shouldn't be any easy way to connect it to you. He just asks that you don't do anything crazy in it."

"I'm not sure it's safe for you two if you're in the Tahoe, either."

"No worries. We've already called to have the Tahoe towed back to the office. We've also booked a week at one of the lodges near Sunset Mountain, in the names of Daniel and Rose Hartman. You roughly match their descriptions. Well, except for..." Iris waved at Risa's pregnant belly. "They're waiting for us at the lodge. You'll drop us off and they'll drive us back home. Then you stay in the lodge in their names."

"The lodge has free Wi-Fi, so you can get online if you need to do any research. And here." Maddox reached into his pocket and pulled out a phone, which he slid across the table to Connor. "No trackers, no connection to Campbell Cove Security or anyone else. Daniel bought it earlier this morning. It's got an app that lets you change your phone number as often as you like, so if you have to make calls, use the app and keep switching out the numbers. That will make you very hard to track."

So far, they hadn't told Maddox about their suspicions regarding the agri-tech firm Risa had been vetting shortly before the plane crash. Connor glanced at Risa and saw the wariness in her hazel eyes. He decided to let her make the decision about what else to tell Maddox.

Apparently she decided to keep those facts to herself for the time being, for she remained quiet through lunch and made only small talk as they exited the sandwich shop into the warming afternoon sunlight.

"Since y'all will be at the lodge through New Year's Eve, if everything goes well, why don't we put the tree on top of the Durango?" Iris suggested. "Most people who stay in the lodges at this time of year are there celebrating the holidays, so it'll add a touch of authenticity."

Connor looked at Risa. Looking genuinely pleased by the idea, she gave a quick nod. "Good idea," he told Iris, and he and Maddox got to work transferring the tree to the Durango's roof rack, while Iris helped Risa pack the rest of their supplies in the back.

"We packed some clothes for y'all," Maddox told Connor when they had finished transferring everything to the Durango.

"I had some maternity clothes left over from my last pregnancy," Iris told Risa. "I'm a little taller than you, but I think they'll fit well enough."

Risa looked up at Connor, her eyes shiny with emotion. She turned back to Maddox and Iris. "I don't know how to thank y'all for everything."

"You'll probably get a chance to return the favor sooner or later, if I know my husband and his history of attracting trouble," Iris said, flashing her husband a look of exasperated affection.

"Here's the wrecker," Maddox said, nodding toward

the large tow truck that pulled into the sandwich shop parking lot. While Maddox and Iris took charge of getting the Tahoe loaded onto the tow truck's flatbed, Connor helped Risa into the front passenger seat of the Durango, then took his place behind the steering wheel.

"Maybe this will buy us enough time to figure out what's really going on," he murmured.

"Maybe." Risa leaned her head against the back of the seat. "I feel as if I'm standing in the middle of a highway with no way to escape. Vehicles flying toward me in both directions, and I don't know which way to turn."

He reached over and took her hand, bringing her knuckles to his lips. He gave them a quick brush of a kiss. "You're not alone in this. We'll figure it out. I promise."

She turned her gaze to meet his, giving his hand a light squeeze. "Don't make promises you can't keep."

"Come on, Risa, have a little faith in me."

The look she gave him was sharp and intense. "I do. I made a big mistake not telling you everything that was happening. I won't make that mistake again."

He wanted to believe her. More than anything in the world.

Iris and Maddox climbed into the backseat of the Durango, snapping the sudden tension that filled the SUV's quiet interior. "All taken care of. You know how to get to the lodges?"

Connor gave a nod, and they were quickly on the road.

"Listen, there's something you need to know."

Maddox broke the comfortable silence that had fallen inside the SUV as they neared the turnoff to Sunset Mountain. "Farid Rahimi is one of ours."

Risa turned around to look at him. "What?"

"Rahimi is one of ours. Working for Campbell Cove Security undercover."

"Since when?" Connor asked, glancing at Maddox's reflection in the Durango's rearview mirror.

"Since the beginning of the company, it seems. He's former CIA. Worked with Quinn for a while at the consulate in Mariposa, under a different name— Malcolm Faris. He's not even Kaziri. He's Iranian. But he spent several years in Kaziristan with Central Intelligence, so..."

Risa shook her head. "Unbelievable. What did Quinn task him to do, act like a complete ass?"

"More or less. He wanted someone in a position to know who's got the power in the Kaziri community in Cincinnati. So they set up the identity of Farid Rahimi and let him play the role from there. He quickly picked up the fact that The Jewel of Tablis was becoming the center of the community, so he and Quinn manufactured him a background and résumé that made him perfect for the management job."

"Did he know who I was?"

"No. Quinn didn't tell him, and apparently you look different enough from your official photos from your previous cover jobs that nobody made the connection."

"Thank God for that," Connor murmured.

"I don't know if it matters now, knowing the

truth about Rahimi. But I thought you had the right to know."

The large wooden sign proclaiming that they'd reached the entrance to Sunset Lodges appeared as they took a sharp curve into a straightaway. Connor slowed the Durango and made the turn through the entrance gates.

"Your cabin is the Big Bear," Maddox told them as they neared the lodge office. He nodded toward a dark blue sedan parked in a space at the side of the building. "That's Daniel and Rose. No need to stop and chat—just drop us off here and keep going."

Connor slowed to a stop to let Maddox and Iris get out of the Durango. He met Maddox's gaze. "Thank you for everything."

"Be safe." Maddox joined his wife and headed for the parked sedan.

Connor drove on, up the gravel-paved road marked "Big Bear Cabin." The road wound up the mountain, ending at a two-story chalet-style cabin nestled in the woods.

"Beats the hell out of the Rest Stop Motor Lodge," Risa said.

With a fervent nod of agreement, Connor parked the Durango and started unloading their things.

Chapter Thirteen

The Christmas tree filled most of the large picture window that, during daylight, offered a splendid view of the fog-veiled Appalachian Mountains spreading east into Virginia. The homemade ornaments and garland went well with the open-beam walls and ceiling of the cabin, Risa decided, and made herself stop wishing they'd been able to purchase twinkling lights to complete the festive picture.

"I can't believe Christmas is less than a week away," she said as she sank onto the sofa next to Connor, who sat with his socked feet propped up on the coffee table while he used her laptop to surf the web.

Connor set aside the laptop and turned to look at her, lifting one hand to touch her cheek. "I can't believe we're actually going to spend another Christmas together."

She leaned closer, and he wrapped one arm around her shoulder, tugging her against his side. They sat quietly for a while, looking at the tree, content not to speak.

"I called Quinn on the burner phone while you were taking a shower," he said a few minutes later.

She looked up at him. "Did you change the number with the app afterward?"

"Yeah."

"What did Quinn have to say?"

"He said we made the right choice, but I could tell he wasn't that happy about it."

"Do you care?" she asked.

He grinned. "Not really."

"Does he have any new information for us?"

"I didn't bring up some of the things we discovered," Connor admitted. "I didn't know if you'd want me to."

"I'd really like to know why Farid—or Malcolm, or whoever he is—took the chance of blowing my cover when he talked my landlord into letting that guy in my apartment. What if it really was Tahir Mahmoud? What if he'd killed me right there in front of Malcolm? Would he have let Tahir kill me in order to protect his own cover?"

"I don't know. But the first chance I get to talk to Quinn face-to-face, you'd better believe I'm going to ask him."

Risa nestled closer to Connor. "I can't shake the feeling that whoever wants me dead is somehow connected to Akwat."

"How could it be connected? All you were doing was a background check."

She rubbed her belly, where the baby was kicking

lightly against her womb. "Well, yeah, it was just a background check at first. But I did start to make a few deeper inquiries."

He looked down at her. "What kind of deeper inquiries?"

"Honestly, it was probably just my paranoid nature, but it occurred to me that if the hemorrhagic fever the bats were incubating in those caves could somehow be coaxed into jumping species, it might turn out to have—strategic implications."

"Coaxed? You mean, on purpose?"

"Maybe."

He frowned, his gaze moving toward the window. He stared at the Christmas tree in silence for a moment. She had a feeling his mind was nowhere near this cozy little living room.

He finally spoke again. "But if the disease jumped species, the bad guys couldn't be sure that they could control the infection."

"That's kind of what I was looking into," she said. "I wanted to see if the disease DNA was close enough to the hemorrhagic fevers we're already familiar with. Maybe something that could be controlled before the effects became pandemic. Bad guys wouldn't necessarily want to wipe out the world's population. In fact, an epidemic wouldn't be necessary to spread terror. You know the kind of hype that accompanied that Ebola outbreak in the US a few years ago, and those cases amounted to almost nothing."

"But imagine if someone were able to spread a

new, unknown virus in a deliberate, controlled way." Connor shook his head, a light shiver rippling through him. "The panic alone could be devastating."

"Exactly the sort of panic terrorism is intended to create."

He turned to face her. "But we're going on the premise that someone in our own government is gunning for you. The US isn't in the terror business."

"No, but what if someone inside the government wants to get their hands on this pathogen first? To weaponize it for his own purposes?"

"What purposes?"

"Any number of things—manipulate the stock market? Undermine trust in public health services? Or private health services, for that matter. Or maybe target a particular population to foment racial unrest."

"God."

"Yeah. Exactly."

Connor laid his head back against the sofa cushions, gazing up at the ceiling. He looked as shaken as she felt. "And you really think it's possible?"

"I was in the CIA long enough to realize that most of our worst-case scenarios weren't nearly bad enough. Look at what happened with Barton Reid. The man was making backroom deals with terrorists in order to manipulate public opinion and legislation that would suit his personal desires. Don't you think he'd have done something just this ruthless if it had served his purposes?"

"But Barton Reid is in jail."

"He wasn't the only person involved in that mess. We know that much from the post-arrest Senate hearings."

Connor rubbed his chin. "You know who we really need to talk to? The people who took Barton Reid down."

"The Coopers," Risa murmured.

Connor nodded. "The Coopers."

CARA COOPER WAS the world's most adorable six-month-old. Wavy dark hair like her mother's and her father's bright blue eyes made her impossible to resist, even on a bad day.

And today had been a very bad day, thanks to the first baby tooth trying to make its way into her toothless little mouth.

Jesse Cooper's cell phone ringing was barely audible over Cara's fretful wails. Evie patted the baby's back soothingly and nodded for her husband to go take the call.

He didn't recognize the number displayed on his phone, but after an hour of trying to help his wife soothe their little darling, even a crank call would provide a welcome distraction. He closed the door behind him, muting the baby's cries, and answered the phone. "Jesse Cooper."

"Mr. Cooper, my name is Connor McGinnis. I work for Maddox Heller."

Ah, Jesse thought. His former partner strikes again. "How's Heller these days?"

"Seems well," McGinnis answered, his tone suggesting he was running low on patience.

So Jesse cut to the chase. "What do you need?"

There was a brief pause, as if Jesse's blunt question had caught McGinnis by surprise. Then the other man outlined the reason for his call in the sort of quick, organized spiel that told Jesse that Connor McGinnis was, like Jesse himself, a product of the US military.

"So, you want to know if any of Barton Reid's associates could still be pulling strings inside the government?" Jesse summed up.

"Yes."

"Short answer, yes. It's possible." He and his family had done a lot to limit the damage Barton Reid did to American influence in the Middle East and Central Asia, and to thwart his group's domestic terrorism ambitions. They had helped authorities apprehend and convict the worst offenders, but Jesse had never lost sight of the fact that there were probably others like Barton Reid out there, lying low, waiting for a chance to make another move.

"Possible," McGinnis repeated. "But you don't have a handy list of suspects, I take it?"

"No. But if you think that's what you're up against, I might be interested in looking into the matter." He had a few resources inside the government he could turn to. Plus, his gruff father-in-law, retired US Marine Corps General Baxter Marsh, knew where a whole lot of bodies were buried at the Pentagon.

If someone was planning to use a position high in the US government for his or her own benefit, it would give Jesse a great deal of pleasure to put a permanent stop to the plot.

"I'm not really able to come down there and discuss it with you." For the first time in the phone call, McGinnis sounded tentative, even wary.

"Are you the person with a target on your back?" Jesse asked.

"No."

But maybe it was someone he cared about, Jesse thought. "Why haven't you taken this to Heller? Isn't he working for some government security contractor now?"

"He is. So am I."

"But contacting the company could be dangerous to you?"

McGinnis didn't respond. It was all the answer Jesse needed.

"Okay. I can come to you," Jesse said finally. "But I'll have to talk to Heller first. Make sure you're on the level."

"Are you sure you want to get that involved in this situation? Maybe this is something we could just discuss over the phone. It would be safer that way. For you, at least." From McGinnis's tone, Jesse could tell that the situation might be even more dire than he thought.

But he'd been in some grim tangles before and lived to tell about it.

"I spent over a decade in uniform risking my life to protect the citizens of the United States," Jesse said. "I didn't stop doing that when I finally took the uniform off."

"Neither did I."

"Then you know what I mean. You're talking about a plot to deliberately infect people with a deadly disease in order to create panic and terror. I can't let that stand if I can do something about it."

"I know," McGinnis said grimly. "But all I'm working with right now is suppositions. What-ifs."

"So let's try to find something a little more concrete," Jesse said.

DEEP NIGHT HAD fallen over the mountains, and with it, the first flutterings of new snowfall. Just flurries at the moment, but even inside the cabin, warmed by central heat and a crackling fire, Risa felt the unmistakable chilled, damp promise of more snow.

"I don't know if this is a good idea." She turned to look at Connor, who was crouched by the hearth, stoking the fire as if he, too, felt the gathering fury of winter.

"I don't, either." He stood and crossed to where she stood at the big picture window, gazing past her own faint reflection to the dusting of snow starting to gather on the wooden deck outside. "But we can't just hunker down here forever. You're—we're—about to have a baby. I don't want Junior to come into the world with a target on his own little back."

"Or hers," Risa murmured, turning toward him as he moved closer.

He pulled her into an embrace as if it were the most

natural thing in the world. And it had been, once. As natural as breathing.

She nuzzled closer. "When's he supposed to arrive?"

"If the weather cooperates, tomorrow afternoon. Apparently Cooper Security has their own chopper."

"Unfortunately, I think we're getting more snow sooner or later."

"Hopefully later." He tangled his fingers in her hair, gently tugging until she looked up at him. "Meanwhile, let's think about something pleasant, okay?"

She flattened her palm over his chest, enjoying the feel of his heartbeat beneath her fingers. "Like what?"

"Like, have you thought about names for Junior?"

She hadn't, she realized. Was that strange? She'd tried out numerous nicknames over the past few months, as her pregnancy went from little more than a notion and slight thickening of her lower belly to the reality of stretch marks, cravings, weight gain, and something alive and kicking inside her.

"No," she admitted. "I haven't."

"Why not?"

She looked up at him and blurted the truth she hadn't even realized herself. "I think I was hoping we could choose a name together."

For a second, she thought he was going to pull away from her at the stark reminder of the way she'd failed him. But his expression shifted, a smile flirting with his lips. "Knew you couldn't stay away from me forever, huh? That old McGinnis mojo in overdrive."

She gave a surprised laugh and punched his shoulder. "Conceited ass."

He lowered his head, resting his forehead against hers. "That's half my charm, darlin'."

She rose to her toes and kissed him, just a delicate brush of her lips on his, but sparks seemed to crackle between them on contact, and Connor sucked in a swift breath.

Then he kissed her back, and there was nothing delicate about it. She met his fierce passion with equal fervor, curling her fingers through his hair and pressing her body against his, straining to get closer. Each caress seemed born of storm and fury, as if months of need and longing, pent up to the point of bursting, had breached a dam and spilled over, swamping them with need.

He took her hand and began moving toward the bedrooms. They stopped at the nearest one, the one she'd chosen as her own. Tripping over one of her discarded shoes, they stumbled into the bed, laughing as they almost slid into the floor.

In a way, stripping his shirt over his head and reaching to unzip his jeans seemed like the most natural thing in the world to Risa. She knew his body almost as well as she knew her own. The scar on his shoulder, thick beneath her fingers, was a near miss from the Battle of Fallujah. The thin scar on the back of his hand was from a Taliban soldier's knife, wielded in hand-to-hand combat in the Helmand province of Afghanistan.

And the bullet furrow just over his hip had come

nearly a decade ago when al Adar rebels took the US Embassy in Tablis, Kaziristan, in a three-day siege.

He caught her face between his hands, gazing into her eyes as if he was seeing her for the first time. Maybe, in a way, he was. He'd never seen her face filled out the way it was from her pregnancy. And there were new marks on her body as well, stretch marks around her hips and belly. Her breasts had grown a cup size, and her bottom was a lot curvier than he would remember.

Slowly, he tugged her sweater over her head and dropped it over the side of the bed, taking a moment to simply look at her. His gaze dropped to her breasts, straining against the too-small bra that Iris Heller had lent her. Downward, taking in the round swell of her pregnant belly, the road map of stretch marks and the button of her navel.

She felt suddenly self-conscious in a way she had never felt with him, nearly overcome with the urge to cover herself, to hide the changes in her body from his too-sharp eyes.

As she reached for the blanket, he caught her hand. "Don't."

She waited, heart pounding, as he smoothed his hand across her belly, his fingertips tracing a shivery path over the curves. The baby gave a sharp kick against Connor's palm, making him grin.

"You are so beautiful," he said, bending to kiss her belly. Then, his beard stubble rasping against her stomach, he lifted his gaze to her and grinned. "You, too."

God, she loved him. More than she had ever realized.

RISA CURLED UP like a kitten in her sleep, her naked backside tucked in the curve of his body, soft and deliciously warm. Connor pulled her against him, feeling a powerful need to shelter her from the world outside the walls of the cabin, a concept she would laugh at if he ever spoke it aloud.

She was, as he knew, supremely capable of protecting herself. She'd managed to stay alive with very little protection for seven months with a price on her head, after all.

But she was his wife. The other, vital part of his heart. He'd thought she was lost to him forever, and now that he'd had time to work through all the reasons she'd hidden the truth from him for as long as she had, he knew whatever mistakes she'd made weren't significant compared with the possibility of losing her again.

He had to find out who had targeted her. Find a way to put an end to the threat, once and for all.

And that meant finding out why there was a price on her head in the first place.

"You still awake?" Risa's sleepy voice was a soft murmur in the quiet darkness.

"Mmm-hmm," he answered.

"Do you think I'm fat?"

He laughed softly. "You don't really expect me to answer that question, do you?"

"Does that mean you do think I'm fat?"

He gave her backside a light slap. "I think you're perfect."

She made a soft, purring noise. "That's such a good answer."

He grinned. "I missed you so damn much."

She was silent for so long, he thought maybe she'd drifted back to sleep. Then she rolled over to face him, cupping his jaw with her palm. "I missed you, too. Every single minute of every single day."

He kissed her brow. "We've got to figure out who's trying to kill you."

"First we have to figure out why. That'll tell us who." A soft grumbling noise rose between them, and she grinned. "The kid and I are hungry."

He wrapped a piece of her dark hair around his finger. "We never got around to dinner, did we?"

She sat up and started scooping up clothing. "Beat you to the kitchen!"

By the time he pulled on a pair of jeans and padded barefoot into the kitchen, Risa was bending to look inside the refrigerator. "It was very sweet of Rose and Daniel to buy some groceries for us."

"We need to start adding up all the money we're going to owe people when this is over," he said.

"I know." She pulled out a package of sliced roast beef and a small jar of mayonnaise. "Roast beef sandwiches?"

"Sounds good to me." He found the loaf of bread in

the box by the refrigerator and pulled out a few slices. He started to put two pieces in the toaster for her before he remembered that pregnancy could change a woman's food preferences. "Toasted or not?"

"Toasted," she said with a quick grin. "You had to ask?"

"Didn't know if Junior in there preferred it a different way."

"Ah." She smiled. "I've been lucky. Junior hasn't really changed any of my tastes."

"No cravings?"

"Oh, I've had cravings. But I just crave stuff I already like. Chocolate. Salt-and-vinegar chips." She nodded at the toaster. "And toast."

They lowered the lights and ate at the coffee table in the den, with a view of both the homey Christmas tree and the snow flurries falling in light showers outside, illuminated by the floodlights on the outside of the cabin. Afterward, they curled up on the sofa and flipped channels on the television until they found an old Cary Grant movie they hadn't seen in years.

It was such a normal way to spend an evening, Connor thought as he draped his arm around his wife's shoulder and nuzzled her hair while Cary Grant hid in a dried-out cornfield, chased by a crop duster. Just an ordinary married couple, baby on the way, watching a movie in front of the Christmas tree. It was the life they'd been planning, he realized, before everything had gone so very wrong.

As the movie wound to its exciting end, Risa

stirred in his arms to ask, "Have you ever visited Mount Rushmore?"

He looked at Cary Grant clinging to the rock face between George Washington and Thomas Jefferson. "No. Definitely not like that."

"My dad used to take my mom and me on what he called our America trips," she said with a smile in her voice. "Did I ever tell you about those?"

"I don't think so."

"After we spent those years in Kaziristan while he was on duty, I think he wanted to be sure I remembered I was an American."

"Do you think he's ever suspected you were a CIA agent?" One thing he and Risa hadn't done as a married couple was spend much time with the in-laws, thanks to jobs that kept them overseas so much of the time.

"I think he probably did, but he was always pretty big on the concept of loose lips sinking ships. So he'd never say it out loud, even if he was pretty sure all my trips across the world weren't really about diplomacy."

Maybe once they got clear of this hit-list mess, he and Risa would finally have a chance to get to know each other's families, like real married couples did. His mother would be thrilled that one of her three sons had finally given her a grandchild, he knew. And he had long suspected that beneath crusty old Benton DeVille's drill-sergeant exterior, there lived an old softy who'd spoil the hell out of his grandchild.

But to have any of those things, they first had to survive.

Whatever it took.

Chapter Fourteen

The list was growing longer than Risa had anticipated. She'd been working for the CIA since the year after she'd graduated from college, plucked out of a Foreign Service fellowship program by Martin Dalrymple himself. Her fluency in Kaziri, Farsi and Arabic had made her a valuable asset put to use quickly.

Now, ten years later, she was beginning to realize just how many contacts she'd made during her time in the agency.

"That many, huh?" Connor set a glass of apple juice on the table in front of her and pulled up a chair next to her.

"I really thought it might be easier to figure out who I might have ticked off enough to earn a price on my head." She put the pen down on the table and picked up the coffee mug, curling her cold hands around the warm stoneware. "But apparently there are dozens of people who could want me dead."

"Not everybody on that list has a reason to want you dead, surely."

"That's the real problem," she said. "I could be on

a hit list for reasons I know nothing about. What if someone thinks I saw or heard something that could someday cause a problem? It wouldn't even have to be something obvious to me. It could be something that, eventually, will make sense to me once it all unfolds. And maybe someone doesn't want me to be around when that happens."

"Oh, well. That certainly narrows it down." His tone was dirt-dry.

"I wish we could find out what Dal was thinking."

"A little late for that."

She rubbed her gritty eyes. "Yeah, I know."

His fingers brushed her cheek, making her look at him. His expression was both tender and anxious. "We'll figure this out. Or we'll figure out a way to disappear. I won't let anyone get to you. You know that."

She nodded. "It's just—I don't want to disappear. I've already done it once, and I hated it."

"You won't be alone." His thumb caressed her chin. "Junior and I will be there."

She held his hand against her face. "I know. But I'm going to have a baby. Our parents are going to have their first grandchild. Do you really want Junior to grow up not knowing them?"

She could see the answer in his troubled gaze, before he said the words. "No. I don't."

"I don't, either. So we're going to have to find the answer, not just run away again."

She leaned in and kissed him lightly before pulling away and picking up the pen again. "What did Heller have to say this morning?"

"Not much. He's looking into the death of the agri-tech guys, to see if there's any chance their deaths were anything other than random terrorism, but it can be hard to get information from that part of the world, especially when he's trying to do it anonymously."

"The last thing he needs to do is ping anybody's radar," Risa warned.

"Believe me, I don't want him and his family to be on anybody's hit list, either. But we need information. We can't hide out forever." He reached over and touched her stomach, grinning as the baby gave a sharp kick against his palm. "We've got a kid to raise."

Risa patted his hand. "I wonder if maybe we should be talking to Rebecca Cameron instead of Heller. She's the one who has all the contacts in the State Department. Maybe she might have an idea or two about who might be running something on the side."

"She hasn't been in government in almost five years."

"But she knows a lot of people who are still there."

"I could call Heller back. Suggest he talk to her, tell her what we're looking for."

Good idea, Risa thought. Better to let Heller ask the questions, at least for now. She wasn't sure how well the burner app Connor had downloaded to the phone was going to work if he kept calling people on it.

While Connor wandered off to make the call, Risa looked at the list of names she'd written down. The problem, she realized, was that almost everyone on the list had people they had to report to in some way. And most of those people had bosses as well. Even covert operations had layers of bureaucracy involved, and anyone on any level of the operation could be the person who had put her on the hit list.

And that was assuming she was dealing with someone in the government in the first place, and not al Adar or one of the other terrorist groups she'd gotten crosswise with over the course of her covert career.

Connor returned and sat beside her. "Heller said he'll get Cameron involved. He wants me to call every eight hours to get an update, since he can't call me because I'll be changing the phone number after every call."

"Okay. Good idea," she said, barely listening.

"You're distracted."

She sighed, looking up from the paper. "What if we're chasing shadows here? Dal seemed to think al Adar was who put the hit on me. Maybe we're trying too hard to complicate things when we should be focused on our original belief."

He didn't look happy. "Is this you telling me you want to go back to Cincy?"

"It's where Dal thought I should be."

"And Dal is dead now."

"We could find Farid—Malcolm—whoever he is. Find out what he knows about those men."

"I'm sure Quinn already knows everything he knows about those men," Connor said firmly. "If it's something we need to know—"

"We need to know!" she said sharply. "And Quinn has no right to keep information from us that way. If Heller hadn't figured it out, we still wouldn't know Farid was on your company's payroll. This is our lives, Connor, not just one of Quinn's operations. I don't trust him to tell us what we need to know. Do you?"

"No," Connor said although Risa could tell he didn't like admitting it.

"For the record, I don't think we should go back to Cincinnati," she said with a sigh. "But I do want to talk to Malcolm. If nothing else, I think we need to find out if the man who tried to talk his way into my apartment was really Tahir Mahmoud."

"I can guarantee you, Maddox Heller will be on top of that question."

Risa supposed he was right. If there was anyone in the world who had a better incentive to find out if Tahir Mahmoud was still alive, it was Heller. Not only had he witnessed Mahmoud killing an embassy translator in cold blood during the US Embassy siege a decade ago, he'd also nearly lost his wife to Mahmoud's murderous plot.

"Okay. So we leave that to Maddox Heller."

"I did some digging on the murder of Martin Dalrymple," Connor added. "Still no idea who killed him, but the postmortem results suggest he was killed forty-eight hours before his body was found."

"Which means whoever tried to contact me Wednesday morning wasn't Dal." She frowned. "Do you think that means he was killed because he was trying to protect me?"

"You're not blaming yourself, are you?"

"No," she lied.

He caught her hands in his, making her look at him. "Dal is the person who put you in this situation, which means he knew the score. He made his choices knowing the potential consequences."

"I wish he'd told me more about what he was investigating. I should have asked more questions." The problem was, she'd been taught not to ask questions. Dal had always told her just what she had needed to know. No more, no less.

Without his direction, she felt as if she were stumbling around, blind.

A good way to end up dead.

JESSE COOPER ENTERED the Sunset Mountain Grille at three on the dot and went to stand near the restrooms, as Connor had suggested. He wasn't a particularly large man, which somehow caught Connor by surprise. Though it shouldn't have—some of the toughest marines he knew had been average-sized. What he lacked in size, Jesse made up in sheer presence. He was lean and fit, his dark hair cut high and tight, as if he hadn't really left the Marine Corps behind when he retired.

Connor approached him slowly, giving the man

time to see him coming. Jesse's dark eyes followed him in, his gaze assessing. "McGinnis?"

"Cooper." Connor extended his hand.

Jesse shook it with a firm grip. "Good to meet you."

Connor nodded for Jesse to follow him to the table near the back where Risa waited. Jesse gave her a nod of greeting and took the seat across from her, while Connor sat beside her.

"I was intrigued by what you told me on the phone," Jesse said as soon as a waiter took their drink orders. "I had some of my people do some digging, and it seems that your thoughts about a potential bio-weapon aren't out of the question. Terrorists, whether foreign or domestic, would love nothing more than to use diseases to spread terror. We saw it after 9/11 with the anthrax letters. There's some fear that terrorists might be looking for ways to get their hands on the Ebola and Marburg viruses to use to spread fear."

"So, this hemorrhagic fever in the bats that Akwat found could be a potential weapon in the hands of terrorists?"

"Only if it jumps species," Jesse answered. "Which could potentially be hurried along if infected bats were harvested and induced to bite animals like goats and pigs, increasing the likelihood that the disease could jump into those animals. And that would increase the likelihood that humans could eventually be infected, since they're exposed to livestock far more regularly than bats in a cave."

"Right," Risa said with a nod. "Akwat had been

considering applying for a UN research grant to isolate the infected bat colonies and provide them to scientists for research, while separating them from the healthy bat populations that they planned to use to harvest guano for fertilizer."

"Except, now Akwat is no more," Jesse said.

"Right." Risa looked grim. "The question we're considering is, could their deaths be connected to the attempt on my life?"

"Potentially, yes." Jesse lowered his voice and looked at Connor. "A former employee of mine is working at Campbell Cove Security now. Eric Brannon. Do you know him?"

"Not well," Connor admitted. "He's a former navy doctor, right?"

"Right. One of his interests is infectious diseases. I think it's the main reason he joined your company— access to a research grant studying the potential use of infectious diseases as weapons of terror."

Risa looked at Connor. "Did you know about this?"

He shook his head. "It's not my area of expertise."

"But Quinn would know, wouldn't he?"

"Yes," Connor admitted. "He would."

"Quinn and his 'need to know' garbage," she growled.

"Listen—I'll vouch for Eric Brannon. He's a good guy. A man of integrity." Jesse reached into his jacket and pulled out a card. "I wrote his home number on the back of my card. Call him. You can trust him. Heller will vouch for him, too."

Connor glanced at Risa. She was wearing her best

poker face, but he could feel the tension in her leg where it rested against his. "Thank you," she said aloud, taking the card.

The waiter brought their drinks—coffee for Connor and Jesse Cooper, and water for Risa—and asked if they were ready to order. Connor told him they needed a few more minutes and the waiter headed for another table.

"I'm up here for a couple more days. My wife and I needed a little alone time, so we left the baby with my sister and her husband." Jesse grinned. "Meggie just found out she's pregnant, so I thought they should get a sneak preview."

Risa smiled. "I could use one of those. Get ready for Junior."

Connor tamped down a sudden rush of sheer panic. In a month, he was going to be a father.

What the hell did he know about being a father? His own father had only recently retired from the Navy. He'd been away from home as much as he was there, and while he'd loved his children dearly, he hadn't exactly given Connor a hands-on example of how to be a dad.

"It's a lot of work. Not much sleep. But I wouldn't trade it for anything." Jesse smiled. "And believe me, I never thought I'd say something like that."

Connor felt Risa's fingers curl around his beneath the table, her touch comforting. Calming.

"If you want me to be there when you talk to Brannon, let me know. Don't feel obligated to do so, though." Jesse picked up his menu. "Let's eat, shall we?"

DESPITE THE VOUCHING of both Jesse Cooper and Maddox Heller, Connor and Risa agreed that it was wiser to meet Eric Brannon in a public place rather than letting him come to them. Connor made the call and set up a meeting for the next morning at a park a few miles outside of Cumberland.

"I think Quinn just wants us to hunker down somewhere and stay out of his way." Connor tugged her closer under the covers.

Risa flattened her back against his front, enjoying the light rasp of his chest hair against her skin. "I'm beginning to think that's what Dal wanted, too."

"Maybe they're both right. Maybe you should just concentrate on staying safe. You're weeks away from giving birth—this isn't the time to put your life in danger."

"I won't stop being in danger if I lie low." She rolled over to face him. "I want our child to be born in a hospital under his or her real name. I don't want to try to raise a baby while we're constantly on the run."

"I don't want that, either." He brushed her hair away from her eyes, letting his fingers trail across her cheek. Sheer pleasure raced through her where he touched her, and she had to struggle to focus on his words. "But I don't know how to make the danger go away. We don't even know where the danger is coming from."

"I don't think it's from Tahir Mahmoud or whoever that guy at the restaurant was," she said.

"Even after he tried to get inside your apartment?"

"He did that because I followed him. Before that,

I don't think I was on his radar at all. Which means he's not the person who wanted me dead."

"But someone was tracking us, and that tracking started the night we left Cincinnati."

"Exactly. I think the men in the restaurant were coincidences. I think whoever was looking for me had probably been keeping an eye on you while you were in Cincinnati. In fact, they might have been tracking Quinn and other people at Campbell Cove Security as well. You're on the government payroll, which means there are ways for people in the government to track what y'all do."

"So, technically, someone might have already known we spotted you in Cincinnati, and they just waited for me to find you before they made their move." Connor shook his head. "If you're right about that, then whoever's gunning for you is someone inside our own government."

"I can't live like this. I've spent over a decade living my life as someone else. I quit the CIA so I could just be me again." She touched his cheek. "So we could finally be us."

Connor caught her hand and pressed a light kiss to her palm, then rolled onto his back and gazed up at the ceiling. He remained quiet so long that Risa thought he might have fallen asleep.

But a moment later, his voice rumbled in the darkness. "We can't meet with Brannon tomorrow. Not if someone in the government is following employees of Campbell Cove Security."

Risa sat up suddenly. "Maddox Heller met with us

in Cumberland. And drove us here. He's one of your company's management team."

"But he drove us here in his brother-in-law's SUV."

"What if someone connects Iris's brother-in-law to Maddox?"

"I think we'd already be under siege if that were so."

Risa lay in the dark, her skin tingling. Suddenly every moan of the wind in the eaves, every rattle of winter-bare tree limbs brushing against one another, sounded like an invasion waiting to happen.

"What if they're out there right now, preparing to make their move?" she asked in a whisper, waiting for him to tell her she was crazy.

But his only answer was to roll out of the bed and pick up his Ruger from the bedside table.

IF THERE WAS anyone outside the cabin, they were extremely well-hidden, Connor decided after going from room to room in the dark, checking their surroundings through the window. Without night-vision gear and thermal imaging, he couldn't be absolutely sure, but he didn't think they were in immediate danger.

But Risa was right about one thing. If the person who was looking for her was in the government, with access to some of the government's resources and secrets, it would be only a matter of time before they figured out where Risa was hiding.

There was only one option to keep her totally safe. They had to cut all ties to their pasts.

"No," Risa said flatly when he brought up the topic when he returned to the bedroom. She was standing at the window, gazing out into the darkness, her arms wrapped around her body as if she were cold. "That's not a life I want to live. It's not a life I want for my child."

"Our child," he said. "I don't want you or Junior dead, and if this is the only way to be sure you stay alive—"

"It's not. You know it's not. It's not any kind of life to live, looking over your shoulder all the time. I spent the past seven months doing just that, Connor. I don't want to spend the rest of my life that way."

"Then what the hell are we supposed to do?"

She turned to look at him. "We meet with Brannon tomorrow, as planned. Pick his brain about Akwat."

"Even though he's connected to Campbell Cove Security?"

"Your people know they have to be circumspect when they meet with us. I'm sure Heller probably spent hours drumming that fact into Eric Brannon's head." She turned back to the window. "We just have to keep taking precautions. We'll be okay."

He wrapped his arms around her from behind, resting his palms against her belly. The baby wasn't kicking, exactly, just sort of rolling, but the feel of that small life beneath his hands was reassuring. He thought he could stay here, just like this, for the rest of the night.

Until Risa's body went stiff against his, and she uttered a soft profanity.

"What?" he asked, his own nerves instantly on alert.

"There's somebody out there in the woods," she whispered.

Chapter Fifteen

In the darkness, there was a flash of movement. A shape, fractionally darker than the shrouded woods surrounding it, moved laterally from one tree to another. Then there was a second shadow gliding through the dark. And a third.

"Three," he murmured, his brain already going through a checklist of defensive actions. The doors and windows were all locked—he and Risa had made almost a ritual of the lock-checking process.

"Four," she corrected as another shape slipped briefly into view.

"And that's just one side of the cabin."

"So maybe as many as sixteen?" Risa's voice shook a little.

"Maybe. Check the window over the deck. I'll take the bathroom." Connor headed for the roomy bathroom with its enormous tub and separate shower. The window there was set higher on the wall, forcing Connor to pull up the dainty chair that went with the vanity table next to the sink. He peered out the window, looking for more signs of movement. He spotted only one dark-clad figure out this window after watching for several minutes.

He went back into the hall and found Risa returning from the room at the back of the house that overlooked the back deck. "Two," she said quietly. "They seem to be taking position just beyond the clearing."

"I guess we should check the front."

"Let's get dressed first. And armed."

Neither of them needed prodding to dress for warmth. They chose their sturdiest shoes—hiking boots for Connor and a pair of trainers for Risa—and armed themselves with the weapons they had—the Ruger and a folding combat knife from his Marine Corps days for Connor, and the Glock and a canister of pepper spray for Risa. Connor tucked extra ammo for them both in the inner pocket of his fleece jacket as they edged quietly toward the front windows of the cabin.

They had almost reached the front when Connor's cell phone hummed against his hip. Adrenaline spiked through him as he eased back into the middle of the cabin, pulling Risa with him.

He didn't recognize the number on the phone display. Warily, he answered. "Hello."

"Mr. McGinnis?" It was a vaguely familiar male voice. Connor couldn't place it immediately.

"You must have the wrong number."

"It's Jesse Cooper," the other voice said quickly, stopping Connor as he reached for the End Call button.

Connor placed the voice now, but he remained

wary. "Jesse who?" Risa leaned closer to listen, and he lowered his head to hers so she could hear.

"Cooper. We met this afternoon. After our discussion, we received intel from some of our sources in the US government that your location may already be compromised."

"I really have no idea what you're talking about."

"We contacted Maddox Heller by way of a secure channel and he agreed it was time for an extraction."

"Extraction?" Connor eyed the front door. Though it was made of reinforced wood and had a sturdy dead-bolt lock, there was also a four-pane window in the upper half of the solid wood, covered on the inside by simple plaid curtains that blocked their view of the other side of the door, though the curtains were thin enough that light from the outdoor spotlights seeped through the fabric.

Suddenly, he thought he saw a shadow move across the squares of light. Was that a footfall on the wooden porch?

A second later, there was a brisk knock on the front door. Beside Connor, Risa gave a start, and Connor's own heart rate rocketed upward.

"I'm outside your front door right now." Jesse's voice filtered through the whooshing pulse in Connor's ear. "I have assets surrounding the perimeter of the cabin in case something happens before we can extract you safely to a new location."

Connor found his voice. "Extract us? Extract us where?"

"Please answer the door, Mr. McGinnis. I'll explain everything." The call ended abruptly.

"This is insane," Risa whispered.

There was another knock at the door, a little more forceful this time.

Risa looked up at Connor, her eyes wide and glittering in the low light. "What do we do?"

"Cover me," he said, and moved to the front door. Edging to one side, he flicked the curtains and took a quick look outside.

Jesse Cooper stood in the doorway, dressed all in black. A grim smile curved his lips as he spotted Connor.

Connor leaned against the wall and took a couple of bracing breaths, then opened the door. "What the hell, Cooper?"

Jesse shrugged off his heavy jacket as Connor locked the door behind him. Beneath the jacket, Jesse was armed for combat, Connor saw—a Glock in a shoulder holster, and a combat knife similar to the one strapped to Connor's leg. "Sorry for the cloak-and-dagger. I didn't want to risk a call until my people were in place."

"Your people?"

"Heller agreed it was too risky to bring company assets into the mix, since it looks as if Campbell Cove Security has been compromised." Jesse nodded at Risa. "Sorry to handle things this way, without giving you any warning, but we thought the fewer communications flying through the atmosphere, the safer it would be for everyone."

"How many people are outside?"

"I brought a force of ten agents. They're all trained for close combat and asset protection. We know how to get you out of here safely."

"This is moving really fast." Risa's voice was soft but intense. "We met you for the first time this afternoon and now you expect us to just go with you to God knows where on your say-so?"

"I wish I had time to give you the full Cooper Security sales spiel, but I left my PowerPoint files at home," Jesse drawled. "Meanwhile, there may very well be some very dangerous people headed your way."

"How could they have found us?"

"Your vehicle is registered to a rental company, who gave me the name Daniel Hartman as the person who rented the SUV. Got his billing information in the same call, and it took little effort to discover he's married to a woman named Rose Browning Hartman. Rose Browning's name came up on a news search, connecting her to a woman named Iris Browning. Who's married to Maddox Heller, co-owner of Campbell Cove Security."

"You knew all that already."

"That's why I gave the task to one of my researchers, who knows nothing about Heller or the Brownings or anyone else. She came up with the information pretty quickly."

"But you had to know my car tag number to begin."

"You think that information couldn't be reversed? Start with Maddox Heller and start making connections until you found a Daniel Hartman who'd rented an SUV and a cabin in the Kentucky mountains?" Jesse shook his head. "They know about Campbell Cove Security. So anyone connected to your company or the people there is a liability at the moment. Heller agrees."

"Aren't *you* connected to Heller?" Connor pointed out.

"Not anymore. Not for over a year now. It was worth the risk, but we're still using burner phones and vehicles that can't be directly connected to Cooper Security."

"Why are you doing this?" Risa asked. "We can't pay you."

"Let's just say this is personal and leave it at that."

"Because you think it might be connected to Barton Reid?"

"If it is, my company needs to know. We have a long history dealing with Barton Reid and his happy clan of lunatics." Jesse's voice darkened. "I really hate loose ends."

A MALE VOICE crackled over the handheld radio in response to Jesse Cooper's terse query. "East quadrant clear."

"So far, so good," Jesse said as he hooked the radio onto his belt again and leaned his hips against the dresser. "Can I help you with anything?"

"Tell us where we're going, for one thing," Risa suggested, stuffing the last of her borrowed clothes into a rucksack Jesse had supplied, apparently at Maddox Heller's suggestion.

"My brother-in-law and sister are acquaintances of a family who runs a small motel and tavern not far from here," Jesse said, checking his watch. "But there's not a known connection between them, so it should be perfectly safe. They've agreed to rent us a block of rooms for the next few days, no names given, no questions asked. We'll be paying in cash. We'll be traveling in cars rented by people with only the loosest of connections to my family and no connection at all to Maddox Heller or Alexander Quinn."

"You think of everything," Risa muttered.

"I know you two aren't sure you can trust me," he said quietly. "I wish I had time to prove you can. But time is something we just don't have."

Connor zipped up his bag. "I'm done."

Risa closed her bag as well. "Me, too."

"Okay, good. Now, here's where it gets a little harder."

Risa exchanged glances with Connor. "Harder in what way?"

"For this next short trip, we're going to have to separate you."

"No," Risa and Connor said in unison.

"We don't want to go in a full motorcade out of here. It'll be too obvious. I want to split you up so that you'll both have a lead vehicle and a vehicle in the rear. If something goes wrong with one package— the package being each of you—we can still whisk the other package to safety."

"With all due respect to your obvious planning and preparation," Connor said, "Risa and I just spent the past seven months apart. I'm not letting her out of my sight that long again. Not even for an hour."

"I agree with Connor," Risa said firmly.

Jesse pressed his lips into a thin line. "And you won't budge?"

Again they spoke in unison. "No."

A faint smile curved Jesse's lips. "I now owe my wife fifty dollars. She said you'd never go for the splitting up idea."

"Wise woman," Connor said.

"So, there's a plan B, I hope," Risa said.

"Well, it's basically plan A, but instead of there being two packages, there'll be one real package and one decoy," Jesse told them. "My sister Isabel has a similar build and coloring to you, so she was going to play the role of you anyway, if we'd split you up from Connor. Under a coat, with some extra padding, she'll pass for pregnant. Her husband, Ben, looks enough like Connor to make a decent decoy, too. So they'll be the other package."

Risa looked at Connor, not sure she was happy about so many people being in harm's way just to protect her. Dal was already dead. Malcolm Faris might already be in danger because she'd chosen to work at the restaurant where he was already undercover.

Now Jesse Cooper and ten other agents were about to put their lives on the line to protect Risa.

But why? Did they know something they weren't telling her?

"Wait," she said as they reached the front door. "I need to know something."

Both Connor and Jesse turned to her with questioning looks. "We're already running out of time," Jesse warned.

"You know why I've been targeted, don't you?" she asked. "You must know, or you wouldn't have put your people on the line this way. What have you found out? Where are we really going?"

Jesse sighed. "I was going to explain it all when we got there, but yes. I do think I know why you've been targeted. I just don't know who's pulling the strings." He nodded toward the door. "Let's get on the road. I'm your driver anyway, so I'll tell you everything on the way."

Risa looked at Connor, trying to gauge what he was thinking. Were they crazy to trust their lives to a man who was, despite his reputation as a security expert, a stranger to them?

Connor flashed her a smile that she suspected he meant to be reassuring. It might have worked if he'd looked a little less queasy.

But she steeled her spine, took his hand and fell into step with him as they followed Jesse Cooper to the big black Explorer parked outside the cabin.

SUNSET MOUNTAIN WAS one of the few towns in the county with its own police department, a holdover from a time decades ago when it had been one of the larger towns in the area. The Sunset Mountain PD had slowly downsized over the years to its current staff of eight uniformed officers, four detectives, an assistant chief and Chief Kenneth Halsey.

Halsey was a big man, tall and broad-shouldered, his steel-gray buzz cut giving him the air of an aging but still-fit drill sergeant. He knew his time at the head of the police department was limited; already the town council was making a lot of noise about disbanding the department to save money. Sooner or later, they'd vote to turn over policing duties to the county sheriff's department, and Halsey would either have to go to the county boys, hat in hand, in search of a job that probably wouldn't be there, or retire.

But he'd worry about that when the time came. Meanwhile, he had a whole other kind of headache that had just landed on his desk.

"What kind of terrorists are we talking about?" he asked the well-dressed stranger who'd barged into his office a few minutes earlier, asking for help in setting up a roadblock.

"We believe the woman is planning to set off a bomb at Kingdom Come Park as soon as it opens this spring. She's one of those immigrants causing all that trouble up in Cincy."

"Ah." Halsey had heard about the protests. "But weren't those people up there the ones protesting against the terrorists in their country?"

The man, who'd identified himself as Garrett Leland, flashing Department of Homeland Security credentials to prove it, arched his eyebrows as if surprised the police chief knew even that much about the immigrant protests.

What, he thought Halsey was some sort of inbred hillbilly cop who hissed and spat at the mere thought of foreigners in his neck of the woods? Halsey's wife was from Nigeria. His kids were half-black. Ol' Garrett Leland had picked the wrong yokel if he thought he could play the foreigner card.

"She was involved with four terrorist bombings in Kaziristan, and another in France. We believe she's radicalized the father of her unborn child and they should both be considered armed and extremely dangerous." Leland placed a photograph on Halsey's desk. It looked like a security camera image, a little grainy, showing a very pregnant woman wearing a shabby overcoat and a gauzy scarf over her dark hair.

Pretty girl, Halsey thought. Didn't look like a terrorist, but looks could be deceiving. And if there was any chance the woman was up to no good in his neck of the woods…

He released a sigh. "Okay, tell me what you need."

He didn't like the smile that flashed across Garrett Leland's face.

"His name is Garrett Leland," Jesse Cooper said. "He's an agent with Homeland Security."

"You're kidding me," Connor said.

"I wish I were."

"We haven't made a direct link between him and Barton Reid." The speaker was a dark-haired woman with intelligent blue eyes and a quirky smile. Evie Cooper, Jesse's wife. Like Jesse, she was dressed in dark clothes and well-armed, though she confessed, as she buckled herself into the passenger seat, that she worked in Cooper Security's accounting office.

"I train all of my people to handle dangerous situations," Cooper had explained, slanting a proud look at his wife. "Evie can hold her own."

"But you obviously have a reason to think there might have been a link," Risa said.

"He's been on our watch list for a while, but we hadn't really seen any signs that he's working a personal agenda," Evie explained. "But our analysts did some poking around this afternoon after Jesse called in the details of your suspicions about Akwat and the deaths of the two founders. Like I said, he's on our watch list, and you two seemed to think you might be under surveillance by someone with government ties."

"And they found something?" Connor asked.

"About eight months ago, shortly after you filed your preliminary report on Akwat, he requested and received permission to open an investigation into the company's American investors."

Next to Connor, Risa made a skeptical noise in the back of her throat. He couldn't blame her. "That sounds like a fairly reasonable thing for Homeland Security to investigate," he said.

"Which is probably why it didn't ping our radar before now," Jesse said. "But the thing is, he was given carte blanche to form his own investigation team from State, Homeland Security and the Pentagon. And guess what all of the people he tapped had in common?"

A sinking sensation roiled through Connor's stomach. "They were all on your Barton Reid–related watch list?"

"Bingo," Jesse said.

"How did you get this information so quickly?"

"Having the Akwat part of the puzzle speeded everything up. Everything we'd gleaned about the activities of the people on the watch list had been entered into a searchable database. Once we searched for 'Akwat,' the pattern became clear."

Connor rubbed his forehead, where a tension headache throbbed. "That's a lot of manpower for something you're not getting paid to do."

Jesse met Connor's gaze in the rearview mirror. "Who says we're not getting paid?"

"So what makes you think we're in imminent danger?" Risa asked.

"Two hours ago, I made a call to a friend I served with during my Marine Corps days," Jesse answered. "Gunnery Sergeant Ken Halsey, Gunny for short. He's now the chief of police with the Sunset Mountain Police Department. I thought I'd see if he and his wife could meet us for dinner somewhere. But he had to work—some suit from Homeland Security believes there's a terrorist on her way to Kingdom Come Park to scout the place for a terrorist attack once the park opens this spring."

"On *her* way?" Connor echoed.

"Yeah. Seems this woman is a Kaziri. Pregnant and probably traveling with her American lover she's helped radicalize. Ring any bells?"

"Son of a bitch," Connor muttered. "They've come out of the shadows with their search."

"Yeah. And want to take a stab at the name of the Homeland Security suit Gunny was talking about?"

"Garrett Leland," Connor and Risa answered in quiet unison.

"I told him he was looking for the wrong person, and it was important that we got out of town without running into Homeland Security," Jesse said quickly.

"And that was good enough for him?" Risa asked.

"Marine's word," Connor murmured.

"Gunny trusts me, and I trust him—" Jesse's voice cut off abruptly, his body going tense.

"Oh no," Evie murmured, gazing forward through the windshield.

Connor leaned to the center of the SUV and saw the red glow of a string of taillights on the road ahead. Beyond the backed-up traffic, a bank of flashing blue-and-red lights illuminated the scene about a mile away, blocking both lanes.

They'd run into a police roadblock.

Chapter Sixteen

As he tapped the brakes to slow the SUV, Jesse's cell phone rang. Evie answered and listened for a moment, then looked at him. "It's for you." She held the phone to his ear.

Gunny Halsey's gravelly voice rumbled like distant thunder in his ear. He was obviously trying to speak quietly. "We've set up roadblocks on the major arteries in and out of town. Where are you?"

"About to run into one of those roadblocks on Bald Eagle Road."

"How far out?"

"A mile?"

"Anybody behind you?"

Jesse checked the rearview mirror. "No."

"Kill your lights. The taillights ahead should be enough light for you to see Black Creek Road turn-off on the right. Spot it yet?"

Jesse turned off his headlights manually, slowing as he neared the traffic snarl ahead. As his eyes adjusted to the lower light, he spotted the sign to his right. "Got it."

"Take it. It'll be dark as an Afghan cave, but you'll be blocked by trees almost immediately. Put on your parking lights until you think you can risk headlights again."

Jesse slowed into the turn. The glow from the tail-lights on Bald Eagle Road disappeared almost immediately, blocked out by the thick evergreen canopy that closed in Black Creek Road. He decided he could risk the parking lights, which offered a little illumination of the gravel track ahead of him. "Okay, I'm on Black Creek Road. What now?"

"Go until you hit Mill Hollow Road. Take a left and follow it until you hit a T intersection on Grassley Road. From there, take a left and you should be able to get to Cumberland without hitting any of the major roads. Gotta go." Gunny hung up.

Jesse told Evie and the McGinnises where they were going.

"And you trust this Chief Halsey?"

"With my life. Several times, as a matter of fact."

He was far enough into the woods to hit the headlights. They lit up the road ahead, almost painfully bright until his eyes adjusted again.

They drove in silence until an intersection appeared in the gloom ahead, four-way stop signs bringing them to a brief halt. The words *Mill Hollow Road* gleamed in fading fluorescent paint at the corner of the crossroad. Jesse took a left, as Gunny had directed.

Risa broke the silence. "You haven't told us what's

waiting when we get to the motel. Something about a second plan of action?"

"Are you familiar with Senator Gerald Blackledge?" Jesse asked.

"Of course," Risa answered. "He's been a senator since the Lincoln administration, right?"

"He may be a politician down to his bone marrow, but he gives a damn about national security and nothing pisses him off more than corruption in the government. He knows where a lot of the bodies are buried, and he's been instrumental in protecting many of the key witnesses against Barton Reid and his cronies. He's setting up a satellite feed so you can testify to everything you learned about Akwat. You don't have to name names or anything else—just report what you were going to report before your plans were cut short by the plane crash."

"It's going to catch some people by surprise, since your name was on the list of casualties in that crash," Connor said.

"This is good," Risa said. "I think the only reason I've been targeted is because of my unfinished report on Akwat, right? It's the only thing that makes sense, given all the rest of the things we know."

"It seems likely," Jesse agreed.

"It took almost seven months for them to figure out you were still alive and where you might be," Connor said thoughtfully. "I wonder if that's because they managed to get information out of Dalrymple before he was murdered."

"We believe he was working this case off the CIA's

radar, so yeah. If somebody found out I was still alive, it was probably through Dal in some way. Or dumb luck, the way Connor did."

"Do you have the original report somewhere you can access it?" Evie asked, turning around in the seat to look at the McGinnises.

"Yes," Risa answered, the hint of a smile tinting her voice. "I do."

"No sign of them at either checkpoint?" Garrett Leland's accent reminded Ken Halsey of a greenhorn captain he'd been burdened with during a tour of duty in Iraq during the first Gulf War. Complete ass who thought his master's degree in logistics made him God's gift to the Corps. He'd been from somewhere in Massachusetts. Somewhere rich and privileged. His accent was a lot like Leland's. Same attitude, too.

"Afraid not," Halsey answered in the same careful tone he'd used when talking to the idiot captain of yore.

"We've confirmed they've vacated their last known whereabouts," Leland growled, his brow creasing as he started to pace. "We've got the two ways out of town covered. Where the hell could they have gone?"

Another voice piped up. "There's another way out of town, sir."

Alarm rippled down Halsey's spine. He turned to look at the deputy who'd spoken, Josh Phelps, sending him a warning look.

But Phelps was looking at Garrett Leland with

a mixture of awe and eagerness to please. Stupid damn pup.

"What way?" Leland asked.

"There's a back road—Black Creek Road, just off Bald Eagle Road. They coulda seen our roadblock and taken the detour. Black Creek Road takes you to Mill Hollow Road, and from there you can get out of Sunset Mountain without going through either of the roadblocks."

Leland turned to look at Halsey. "You didn't tell me about the detour."

"Nobody except locals know anything about it." Halsey tried not to grit his teeth with frustration. "You said they're not locals."

Leland's expression darkened, and his voice sharpened to a diamond edge. "I said, I wanted to block off every road out of town." He pulled his cell phone out of his pocket and made a call. "It's me. I need a chopper in the air now. Grab a map and find Mill Hollow Road. Make sure every exit off that road is covered. Now!"

Halsey swallowed a profanity. "I'll get you some extra bodies out there to help you," he told the Homeland Security agent, pulling his phone from his pocket. He texted his assistant deputy and gave the order, then pulled up Jesse Cooper's number and typed in a quick message.

Before hitting Send, he glanced up and found Leland watching him, his dark eyes suspicious. Halsey faked a smile. "Should have four more deputies on board in ten minutes. They'll meet your folks at the T intersection off Mill Hollow Road."

He pocketed his cell phone again, but as he slipped it in his pocket, he hit Send.

"OH, HELL."

Evie Cooper's voice roused Risa from a light doze. She looked up to find the woman peering at her husband's cell phone, the light from the display casting blue light across her face.

"Text from Gunny. Leland's ordered a roadblock at the end of Mill Hollow Road."

Risa went from drowsiness to instant alertness. "Can we get there before the roadblock's set up?"

"Unlikely," Jesse answered. "We haven't even reached Grassley Road."

"How big a net are they throwing?" Connor asked. He was on his phone, Risa saw, looking at a map program. "Just the roads?"

"What are you thinking?" she asked.

"We could go on foot," he answered. "Just the two of us, through the woods. Jesse and Evie stay in the SUV and get through the checkpoint. Then we meet back up on the highway past the checkpoint and go the rest of the way to the motel."

Risa saw Jesse and his wife exchange a quick look before he gave a nod. "That could work."

"It's really cold out there." Evie looked worried.

Risa glanced at Connor, smiling. "We've trekked ten miles up a mountain in Kaziristan in winter. We know about dealing with the cold."

"We'll bundle up. Plus, we'll be moving, so that'll keep our body heat up." He was still looking at the map on the phone. "About a quarter mile from the intersection with the highway back to Cumberland, Mill Hollow Road crosses a large creek. If we get out there and start hiking, we can follow the creek to the highway, bypassing the roadblock."

"I'm not sure I like being out of contact that long," Jesse said.

"Do you have another one of those handheld radios?" Risa asked. "We'll have the phone and if we had a radio, we'd have two ways to stay in touch. Then, if something went wrong, we'd know we'd have to come up with a plan C."

"I think this *is* plan C," Jesse murmured. But he waved his hand toward the glove box, and Evie opened it to retrieve an extra radio. She checked the radio's channel setting and handed it to Connor.

THEY CROSSED THE creek and stopped on the other side of the small bridge, pulled over onto the sandy shoulder. There were no headlights visible behind them on the curvy road, but that could change quickly, so Risa and Connor didn't drag their heels. They left Risa's laptop with the Coopers—they'd have no use for it in the woods. Evie had directed them to stow it away in a hidden lockbox tucked under the middle row of seats for just such a purpose. It wouldn't be found in a cursory search, and if the search went any deeper than that, the laptop would be the least of their worries.

Instead, they stashed a change of clothes in a large

rucksack Jesse provided. "There's a first-aid kit, some protein bars and a liter of water in there," he told them as he helped Connor strap the sack to his shoulders. "There are night-vision goggles in there if you need them."

By the time Risa and Connor climbed down the shallow incline to the rocky creek bank, the Coopers were back on the road, their taillights casting a faint red glow over the area for a few brief seconds before they disappeared, leaving them in utter darkness.

Connor retrieved the night-vision goggles and slid them onto his head, adjusting the straps until they fit snugly but comfortably. He was well-accustomed to using the goggles, so adjusting to the green glow of the landscape stretching out ahead of him took only a couple of seconds.

"Just follow me," he told Risa. "I'll let you know if there's an obstacle to worry about, trust me."

"I do," she said with quiet confidence.

He swallowed a smile and started walking.

For a while, they stuck close to the creek bank, avoiding the tangled underbrush of the woods in favor of the clearer, if rockier, path the bank provided. But within a half mile, the creek narrowed considerably, the woods encroaching on the bank until there was no clearing left.

There was no choice but to venture into the underbrush, and their forward progress slowed.

"How're you holding up?" Connor asked Risa as he picked his way around a half-hidden stump in the middle of a tangle of vines.

"I'm okay," she answered, but there was a tightness in her voice that made him turn and look at her.

She smiled at him, her teeth bright through the goggles. But her brow was slightly furrowed, and she had both gloved hands pressed over her stomach.

"Are you sure?" he asked. "You having pains?"

"Just twinges. I've had them before. I'm okay. Let's keep going."

Stopping to argue, he decided, would just prolong their time in the woods. What she needed was a clean bed and full night's sleep. The sooner they rendezvoused with the Coopers, the sooner she'd get what she needed.

They were coming to a part of the creek where the trees and underbrush receded, leaving the bank relatively clear for a long stretch. There was also a fallen tree near the edge of the clearing that offered a tempting place to rest for a few moments. "Let's take a load off for a minute. Get some water."

Risa followed him to the fallen tree trunk and sat, gratefully accepting a drink from the liter bottle of water. "How far are we?" she asked as he flipped up the night goggles and pulled out his phone.

He checked for reception. One bar, but it might be enough to check the map. He pulled up the GPS app and got their current coordinates, then plugged it into the map. "A little over halfway there."

Risa swallowed a sound that sounded a lot like a groan. "Any messages from the Coopers?"

He checked. There was a text message, posted about five minutes ago: Do you want pizza?

"They're at the checkpoint." With any luck, the Coopers would be allowed to pass through the checkpoint unmolested, especially since, during the quick stop to let Risa and Connor out to start their hike, they'd packed away their weapons and firearms—all legally owned and licensed to possess even in Kentucky, Jesse had assured him—in hopes that they wouldn't raise any suspicions. "Hopefully the name Cooper won't trip any alarms."

"I don't know." Risa was rubbing her stomach rhythmically, as if trying to calm both herself and the baby. "If Garrett Leland really is part of the old Barton Reid network of corrupt government employees, I'm guessing he'd be pretty wary of anyone named Cooper."

Connor pulled off his glove and touched her face. Despite the cold, she looked and felt a little flushed. "Are you sure you're okay?"

"I'm okay. Let's just keep going. The sooner we reach the rendezvous point, the better."

He stashed everything back in his rucksack and pulled the goggles down over his eyes, letting them readjust to the night-vision glow. He stood and reached out for Risa's hand, helping her to her feet. "You sure you don't need to rest a little longer?"

"Positive." Her voice sounded stronger. "Let's go."

Over eight months pregnant, he thought. Almost thirty-eight weeks.

Most airlines stopped letting pregnant women fly at thirty-six weeks, didn't they? But here he was, dragging his pregnant wife through the woods in the middle of December.

What the hell was he thinking?

JESSE COOPER'S HEADLIGHTS illuminated the brown-and-tan uniforms of the county sheriff's department, but the man who came to the window, flashlight in hand, was a tall, slim man in a Sunset Mountain Police Department uniform. Lifting his flashlight, he checked Jesse's driver's license, then Evie's. "Alabama, huh? You're a ways from home."

"We're driving north to see my sister for Christmas," Evie said with a friendly smile. "She lives in New York. We decided to make a fun trip of it. Go antiquing, visit some of the sights."

"What's the roadblock for?" Jesse asked, because it was a logical question to ask.

"Just routine," the police officer answered with a polite smile. He handed their licenses back. "Can you lower all your windows?"

"Sure." Jesse depressed the power window buttons, lowering the front and back passenger windows.

The policeman ran the beam of the flashlight through the car, taking in the luggage in the back and the small plastic trash bag hanging on the back of Evie's seat. Jesse knew they'd look like normal travelers. He'd made sure they looked that way.

"All right," the policeman said with a smile. He leaned a little closer and lowered his voice. "Chief Halsey says hi."

Then he stepped back and waved for the others to let them through.

Jesse drove slowly past the small phalanx of deputies and police officers, his pulse pounding like a drum in his ears.

THEY WERE GETTING closer to the highway. Sound carried well in the cold night air, and now and then, Risa heard a vehicle motor, which meant the highway couldn't be that far away now.

The odd sensations in her belly were starting to come more frequently. It wasn't pain, exactly, more a tight rippling sensation in the lower part of her abdomen. It might be muscle spasms, she thought, from the stress of hiking through the woods.

"I think I'm starting to see car lights," Connor said as he pushed his way forward through the undergrowth. They'd had to abandon the creek bank again, slowing their pace as they struggled against the pull of the vines and the constant threat of hidden obstacles under the tangled carpet beneath their feet.

Risa's legs had begun to feel rubbery, and the odd sensation in her stomach was starting to feel less like twinges and more like pain.

Don't think the word, she told herself firmly.

"Definitely seeing lights now," Connor said, excitement and relief coloring his voice. He started to push ahead more quickly now, no doubt spurred on by the prospect of reaching the end of their journey.

Risa followed, struggling to keep up as she refused to dwell on the swelling pain that had started to feel like hard cramps in her lower back and belly. *Don't think the word. Don't think the word.*

Connor slowed to a sudden halt, reaching into his pocket for his phone. He flipped up the goggles and checked his messages. "They got through the checkpoint. They're waiting off the road near the creek crossing."

Relief swamped her, sending a rush of heat pouring down her spine. "Good. Let's go." She put her hand on Connor's shoulder to nudge him forward.

But as she started to take a step forward, a hard cramp shuddered through her stomach, sucking the air from her lungs in a harsh gasp. She grabbed for Connor's arm, doubling over as the pain started to crescendo.

"Risa?" Connor turned to look at her, flipping the goggles up again. His eyes were wide and dark in the gloom.

The pain subsided to a light ache, and she loosened her death grip on his arm. "It's okay. I'm okay."

"No, you're not." His voice was low and shaky. "Are you?"

She could no longer lie to herself. Or to him.

Rubbing her trembling belly, she took a deep breath and said the words she wouldn't even let herself think a few minutes earlier.

"I'm having contractions."

Chapter Seventeen

Do not panic.

Connor's heart had started to race the second Risa uttered the word *contractions* but he hadn't been through years of Marine Corps training and combat experience for nothing. It wasn't even the first time he'd dealt with a pregnant woman, was it? He'd been there when an Iraqi woman gave birth to her fourth child in the back of an armored Humvee. Granted, he'd mostly guarded the vehicle while the team medic handled the push-and-pull stuff, but hadn't he been pleasantly surprised by how smoothly things had gone?

Of course, there was a difference between a fourth baby and a first one, wasn't there? And Risa wasn't some anonymous woman giving birth on the side of the road with the help of a trained medical professional.

She was his wife. Carrying his baby. And depending utterly on him to get her through the next half mile of woods and safely to the waiting SUV.

He had stopped only long enough to pull out his

phone and text a heads-up to Jesse Cooper, then started pulling her through the woods as quickly as they could go.

She had her next hard contraction as they were nearing the highway. As he helped her ride it out, he spotted bits of the blacktop highway through the trees. Less than two hundred yards away.

"Okay," she breathed as the pain ebbed again. "Let's go."

The last hundred yards felt like a nightmare. The hard contraction had passed, but smaller, lighter spasms had Risa panting and groaning as they threaded their way through the thinning underbrush. Finally, they broke through the trees and onto the shoulder of the highway, winter-brown grass crunching beneath their feet.

The SUV was parked about twenty yards from where they emerged, across the highway. Connor ripped off the goggles and waved his arm. The SUV growled to life, the headlights piercing the darkness, and rolled forward to meet them as they hurried across the highway.

Connor lifted Risa into the backseat and climbed in behind her, buckling her in as he gave Jesse an urgent look. "She's had two contractions. About ten minutes apart. How close is the nearest hospital?"

"We can't," Risa said, her voice coming out in soft pants. "I don't have any identification, no insurance—"

"Already taken care of. There's an ob-gyn waiting

at the motel," Jesse said, reaching back to give Risa's hand a quick pat. "We'll be there before you know it."

He might have oversold how quickly they'd arrive at the Meade Motor Inn; Risa rode out a third contraction before they reached the motel, but soon the SUV's headlights illuminated the shabby facade of the motel, giving Connor a brand-new problem to worry about.

"This is where you're proposing that my wife have our baby?" he asked in disbelief. It was a long, one-story building with a boxy office at one end and about twenty small rooms in a row, fronted by a concrete walkway covered by corrugated metal awning held up by rusty steel poles. The place looked as if it had probably been shabby twenty years ago.

"Looks can be deceiving," Jesse said, parking in front of one of the rooms on the far end of the building.

"There's a helicopter in the side lot," Risa said. "Why is there a helicopter?"

"It's for you." Evie turned in her seat and reached for Risa's hand. "The doctor will evaluate your condition and if she feels it's necessary, we'll chopper you to the nearest hospital with a labor-and-delivery unit."

When he entered the room Jesse led them to, Connor saw what Jesse meant when he'd said looks could be deceiving. The room's carpet was a little worn but very clean, the bedclothes neat and spotless. What little he saw of the bathroom before Risa closed herself inside it was also clean and bright.

He turned to Jesse, who had brought their belongings into the bedroom. "Where's the doctor you promised? And who is he?"

"She. And she's in the room next door, with the senator."

Connor stared a moment. "The senator?"

Jesse smiled. "I didn't tell you about the congressional hearing? Senator Blackledge agreed to meet us here and bring some video equipment. We were hoping to have her testify by video to a special panel about her experiences with Akwat and everything that happened after the plane crash." He nodded toward the bathroom. "We didn't count on your wife going into labor."

Risa came out of the bathroom, looking tired and pale. "I can still testify."

Connor put his arm around her and helped her to the edge of the bed, where she sat, bending forward with her hands on her knees. "We can worry about that later. Let's get the doctor in here to take a look at you."

THE OB-GYN WAS an attractive woman in her early fifties named Dr. Andrea Bolling. Besides a pleasant smile and a gentle touch, she possessed a calm competence that went a long way toward easing some of Risa's nervousness. "You're in active labor, and since this is your first, I think we need to get you to a hospital sooner rather than later."

Connor let go of Risa's hand. "I'll go tell Jesse to get the chopper ready to move."

Risa waited until Connor had left the room to ask the doctor, "Are you sure everything is okay?"

"As sure as I can be until we get to a hospital and get an ultrasound done. But from what I can tell, the baby seems to be in the right position, your contractions seem normal, and other than being tired from your recent ordeals, you appear to be healthy. We'll get you through this."

The contractions were getting closer. Only seven minutes between the last couple she'd had. But her dilation was only around five centimeters. From the books she'd read about childbirth, she should still be a few hours away from giving birth.

She went through one more hard contraction before the helicopter was ready to go. Connor and Evie helped Risa out to the black Bell 407 and settled her in one of the five passenger seats. Connor and Dr. Bolling took the seats nearest her, joined by Evie, while Jesse sat in the cockpit with the pilot, a tall, rangy man in his late forties Jesse introduced as his cousin J. D. Cooper.

"We've contacted the Eastern Kentucky Regional Medical Center and arranged for a labor-delivery room to be on standby," Evie told them as they buckled in for the flight. "Courtesy of Senator Gerald Blackledge."

Then the helicopter engine roared to life and it was too loud in the cockpit to hear what anyone had to say.

Connor and Dr. Bolling coached Risa through two more contractions before the helicopter finally came to a landing on the helipad atop the medical center.

An attendant and a nurse were waiting with a gurney to whisk Risa down to the labor-delivery floor. The nurse helped her change into a hospital gown and settled her in a wood-paneled area that strived to look like an ordinary room in someone's home, except for all the medical equipment and the narrow adjustable bed in the center of the space.

Connor entered dressed in a blue coverall gown, a mask hanging around his neck. He took her hand in his. "Ready to get this mission started, Mrs. McGinnis?"

She managed a tired grin. "Ooh rah, Major."

He stroked her hair and looked at Dr. Bolling, who had donned a gown and protective goggles, her hair tucked under what looked like a blue paper shower cap. "I just found out about this a few days ago, so I haven't had time to prep for my part of this job," he told her. "So tell me what to do."

Dr. Bolling's smile crinkled the skin around her soft gray eyes. "In my experience, your best bet is to treat your wife as a queen. She's in charge. Do whatever she tells you she needs."

The look Connor gave Risa made her heart contract. "It'll be my privilege."

"TROUBLE INCOMING."

Evie's voice drew Jesse's attention away from his phone, which he'd been using for the past hour to coordinate with the senator's team as well as his own assets still in Kentucky. Everyone from Cooper Security had made it through the roadblocks unaccosted to reach the motel.

Following his wife's gaze down the hallway outside the delivery suite, Jesse released a gusty sigh.

He should have known everything was going too smoothly.

A tall, officious-looking man in a neat charcoal suit strode down the corridor as if he owned the place, flanked by a small army of uniformed officers and a couple of men who reeked of "federal law enforcement agent."

Wearily, Jesse rose to stand in front of the delivery suite door.

"Who are you?" the officious man asked in an impatient, imperious tone. Garrett Leland, Jesse guessed a moment before the man reached into his jacket and pulled out a small wallet containing his Homeland Security credentials.

"Jesse Cooper," Jesse answered.

"Why are you here?"

Jesse felt his anger rise. "Why are *you*?"

"That's none of your business."

"Exactly."

Leland's mouth flattened to a thin, angry line. He nodded toward the two men who stood at his sides. "These gentlemen are with the FBI."

Jesse nodded at them. "Nice to meet you."

One of the two men shot Jesse a look of mild amusement, but the other continued to look grim and imposing.

"Where is Parisa McGinnis?" Leland asked.

There was no point in lying. "In the delivery suite, having her baby."

Leland nodded toward the door. "Get out of the way."

"You never did say why you were here," Jesse said, keeping his tone conversational, even as he refused to budge.

"This is a federal investigation."

The door behind Jesse opened, and Connor nudged him aside, taking Jesse's place. He closed the door behind him and gave Garrett Leland a glowering look. "This is a hospital. My wife is in labor. I don't care who you are or why you're here, you will remove yourselves from this corridor until after she's delivered. Do you understand?"

Behind Jesse, Evie cleared her throat deliberately. He looked at her, and she nodded toward the nurse's desk, where a silver-haired man dressed in a dark gray suit and crimson tie stood with his own entourage. One of the men beside him was holding a large brown teddy bear, while another was carrying a small potted plant.

Jesse grinned as the silver-haired man spotted the clump of uniforms down the hall. The old man began to walk with a strong, purposeful stride toward them, his entourage following in his wake.

"Major McGinnis!" The man's bombastic drawl carried down the hall. "How is your lovely wife?"

A look of pure loathing twisted Garrett Leland's face, but he schooled his features quickly as he turned to face the newcomer. "Senator Blackledge. How unexpected."

Gerald Blackledge pulled up short of the man from Homeland Security, his thick silver eyebrows notching upward with mild disdain. "Well, of course it was. I took great care to keep my trip here under wraps." He turned his attention to Connor. "I hope all is well with Mrs. McGinnis?"

"So far, so good, Senator."

"Wonderful. My committee so looks forward to hearing from her as soon as she's well enough to speak to us."

"Senator, I'm afraid Mrs. McGinnis is under arrest."

"Nonsense." Blackledge waved off the notion with one hand. "Mrs. McGinnis is a national hero. I believe if you'll check in with the secretary of Homeland Security, you'll find that your precipitous trip to the lovely state of Kentucky was for naught. The warrant for Mrs. McGinnis's apprehension was a dreadful misunderstanding. She is, in fact, a vital part of the Senate's investigation into governmental corruption."

Leland didn't hide his fury. "You're overstepping your bounds, sir."

Blackledge took two strides forward, until he stood directly in front of the man from Homeland Security. "And you, Mr. Leland, have dug your own grave."

Leland was half a head taller than Blackledge, and at least three decades younger, and for a moment, Jesse thought the man from Homeland Security was about to take a swing at the senator. But when the two FBI agents who'd accompanied him to the hospital stepped away and joined the ranks of the senator's entourage, leaving Leland standing in the midst of several confused-looking Kentucky lawmen, the younger man soon realized he'd been beaten.

He started to leave, then stopped and slowly turned to look at Connor. "This is not over."

Connor's lips curved into a feral smile that gave even Jesse a chill. "You're right. It's not."

As Leland began to walk away, a growl of pain erupted inside the delivery suite. Connor hurried back through the door, shutting out all the drama behind him.

Evie sidled closer to Jesse, slipping her hand into his. "I can't believe I'm about to say this, given what a whiny little pain in the backside she's been for the past week, but I can't wait to get back home to Cara."

Jesse pictured his little daughter's scrunched-up, reddened face—Cara Cooper at her imperious worst—and smiled. "Me, either."

"SHE'S BEAUTIFUL," CONNOR BREATHED, one large finger brushing delicately over the newborn's wrinkled red forehead.

Risa took in the slightly misshapen head, the toothless maw opened wide and emitting soft bleats, the reddened skin and squinty eyes, and murmured her agreement. "The most beautiful thing I've ever seen."

Connor met her tired gaze. "I wouldn't go that far. Her mother's just as beautiful."

Risa laughed. "This must be that post-childbirth temporary euphoria thing I've heard about."

The nurse approached with a rueful smile. "Dr. Sankar, our neonatal specialist, wants to give her a full examination since she's a couple of weeks early, so I need to take her to the neonatal unit for a bit. Why don't you try to sleep, Mrs. McGinnis? If everything is okay, I'll bring her back before you know it."

With reluctance, Risa released the infant into the nurse's care, reaching for Connor's hand. "Do you think you could go with her? After everything we've just gone through, I don't like letting her out of our sight."

He gave her hand a squeeze. "I'll see what I can do."

Risa tried to relax, her body aching with overall weariness, beyond the physical ordeal of giving birth. She knew she was probably being overly anxious— the hospital was one of the best in the state, and everyone she'd talked to during her labor had assured her there was ample security in the neonatal unit as well as the nursery.

Connor was back a minute later. "Quinn is here."

Risa frowned. "Why aren't you with the baby?"

"They wouldn't let me go into the neonatal unit, but Quinn brought Eric Brannon, so he suited up and went to stand guard. He has a license to practice medicine in Kentucky, so it's sort of a professional courtesy thing, apparently."

"Are you sure we can trust him?"

"Maddox Heller says yes, and I trust Heller."

She caught Connor's hand, tugging it up to her chest. "And I trust you."

Connor pulled up a chair and sat by the bed, leaning closer. "I love you."

"I love you." She touched his face, relished the rasp of his beard growth against her fingers. "We have a daughter."

His smile was like sunlight. "We do."

"What do you want to name her?"

"I haven't given it much thought," he admitted with a soft chuckle. "I didn't know I was going to be a father until a few days ago, and I was a little preoccupied with other issues."

"I have to admit, I really thought she was going to be a boy." She sighed. "So most of my best name ideas were boy names."

"We could name her after your mother."

She made a face. "Nazina? My mother doesn't even like her name that much."

"My mother?"

"You know I love Shirley, but…"

Connor grinned. "It's a little dated."

"One of the boy names I liked was Kyle," she said, stifling a yawn. "Maybe we could feminize it. How does Kylie sound?"

He tried it out. "Kylie McGinnis."

"Flows well."

He smiled. "It does. Kylie Parisa McGinnis."

Risa wrinkled her nose. "We'll work on the middle name."

He bent and kissed her forehead. "Get some sleep.

Kylie will be back in here, looking for an early breakfast before you know it."

Sinking a little deeper into her pillows, Risa closed
her eyes and dreamed.

Epilogue

Christmas morning came complete with a light dust-ing of snow outside the Sunset Lodges cabin where Connor and Risa had returned after she and tiny Kylie were released from the hospital. She'd given two hours of testimony by video feed from the Meade Motor Inn to Senator Blackledge's panel shortly after she and the baby had been cleared to leave the hospi-tal, then joined a convoy of both Cooper Security and Campbell Cove Security Services agents back to the mountain cabin still booked through New Year's Eve.

"Your apartment isn't set up for a new baby," Mad-dox had told Connor when he bundled them into the Durango for the trip back to Sunset Mountain. "Iris is going to go shopping for the things you'll need back home. I think Evie Cooper's got you covered until New Year's Eve at the cabin. Just relax. Enjoy Christmas with your family."

By family, it turned out, Maddox had meant more than just Risa and their newborn. Connor's parents as well as Risa's were waiting for them at the cabin. Nazina and Benton DeVille were in tears at their first sight of the daughter they thought they'd lost, but it didn't take long for them to transfer a large chunk of their joy to their introduction to their first grandchild.

The past few days had been chaotic, if full of joy, but Connor was happy that he and little Kylie were the first ones up on Christmas morning.

He soothed the mewling infant as he carried her into the large living room, where the first glow of sunrise tinted the eastern sky. The Coopers had gifted them with more than just the baby gear they needed for Kylie while they were staying in the cabin. They'd also trimmed the tree with small, sparkling lights that glowed like stars in the gray morning light when he flicked the power switch.

"I don't think you can see the twinkles yet, baby girl, but one day, when you see a big tree like this, decorated with lights and garland, you're going to be overcome with happiness." He kissed the fuzzy crown of her head. "And greed. But we'll deal with that when it happens."

"Life lessons with Daddy?" Risa's raspy voice made him turn toward the doorway, where he found her mussed and sleepy-eyed, leaning against the wooden frame.

"Something like that." He watched with sympathy as she hobbled toward him, still a little sore from the birth. "Did you get any sleep?"

"Yeah, I got some. You?"

"Some." He rubbed his cheek against Kylie's head. "I guess it's Mommy time, baby girl. She's the one with the milk."

Risa settled in the padded rocking chair near the window and reached for Kylie. Connor handed her over and perched on the window seat beside the rocker while she unbuttoned the front of her nightshirt and guided Kylie to her breast.

With greedy grunts, the baby began to feed, and Risa lifted her gaze to Connor's. "I'm trying really hard to relax, but it's difficult to shake the feeling that I need to be running and hiding."

"I know. You've been at it a long time. But everyone we talked to agreed that you should be safe, now that you've given your testimony. And Campbell Cove Security is going to give us protection for a few weeks, just to be sure."

"I wonder if my testimony is enough to stop whatever Garrett Leland and his cohort were planning for Kaziristan." Risa frowned. "Every time things seem to be going the way of the democratic reformers, something always happens to set them back."

"Rebecca Cameron told me she's going to be heading a task force at Campbell Cove Security to look a little deeper into what happened with Akwat. She asked me if I thought you'd like to be part of that task force."

"You mean work for them?"

"It's a good place to work. We're doing important things there."

She looked down at Kylie. "I can't make that decision right now. All I can think about is our little family."

"There's time."

She looked up at him, her eyes sparkling with tears. "I'm really happy our families are here to share this Christmas with us, but I sort of wish it was just us. We have so much to talk through."

He didn't pretend he didn't know what she meant. "You know, I think we could get ourselves tangled up in all the mistakes and all the choices we made, right or wrong. We could turn this whole thing into a bigger mess without much trouble."

Risa made a face. "I don't want that."

"So let's not. I just need to know one thing. Do you love me?"

She touched his hand where it lay on his knee. "God, yes."

"And I love you."

She gave his hand a squeeze. "I know."

"We want to be together as a family. You, me, Kylie and whatever children we might have in the future, yes?"

She smiled, tears sparkling in her eyes. "Yes."

"Then let's make it happen. Whatever it takes." He leaned over and kissed her, then brushed his lips across Kylie's head. "It's always been how we do things, isn't it?"

She touched his face, her fingers soft but strong. "Yes." Then she pulled him toward her for a longer, deeper kiss.

The sound of stirring down the hall filtered through Connor's haze of happiness. The rumble of his father's voice made him smile and groan at the same time. "Grandparent alert."

Risa laughed softly. "Don't complain. We might be glad to have them hovering around once the sleep deprivation starts to kick in."

Giving Risa one more swift kiss, Connor turned to wish his parents happy Christmas.

The best Christmas ever.

* * * * *

Campbell Cove Academy is just heating up!
Look for THE GIRL WHO CRIED MURDER,
the newest book in award-winning author
Paula Graves's miniseries
CAMPBELL COVE ACADEMY,
available next month.

You'll find it wherever
Harlequin Intrigue books are sold!

Every cowboy has a wild side—
all it takes is the right woman to unleash it...

Turn the page for a sneak peek of
BLAME IT ON THE COWBOY,
part of USA TODAY *bestselling author*
Delores Fossen's miniseries
THE McCORD BROTHERS.

Available in October 2016
only from HQN Books!

LIARS AND CLOWNS. Logan had seen both tonight. The liar was a woman who he thought loved him. Helene. And the clown, well… Logan wasn't sure he could process that image just yet.

Maybe after lots of booze though.

He hadn't been drunk since his twenty-first birthday, nearly thirteen years ago. But he was about to remedy that now. He motioned for the bartender to set him up another pair of Glenlivet shots.

His phone buzzed again, indicating another call had just gone to voice mail. One of his siblings no doubt wanting to make sure he was all right. He wasn't. But talking to them about it wouldn't help, and Logan didn't want anyone he knew to see or hear him like this.

It was possible there'd be some slurring involved. Puking, too.

He'd never been sure what to call Helene. His long-time girlfriend? *Girlfriend* seemed too high school. So, he'd toyed with thinking of her as his future fiancée. Or in social situations—she was his business associate who often ran his marketing campaigns. But tonight Logan wasn't calling her any of those things. As far as he was concerned, he never wanted to think of her, her name or what to call her again.

Too bad that image of her was stuck in his head, but that was where he was hoping generous amounts of single-malt scotch would help.

Even though Riley, Claire, Lucky and Cassie wouldn't breathe a word about this, it would still get around town. Lucky wasn't sure how, but gossip seemed to defy the time-space continuum in Spring Hill. People would soon know, if they didn't already, and those same people wouldn't look at him the same again. It would hurt business.

Hell. It hurt *him*.

That was why he was here in this hotel bar in San Antonio. It was only thirty miles from Spring Hill, but tonight he hoped it'd be far enough away that no one he knew would see him get drunk. Then he could stagger to his room and then puke in peace. Not that he was looking forward to the puking part, but it would give him something else to think about other than *her*.

It was his first time in this hotel, though he stayed in San Antonio often on business. Logan hadn't wanted to risk running into anyone he knew, and he certainly wouldn't at this trendy "boutique" place. Not with a name like the Purple Cactus and its vegan restaurant.

If the staff found out he was a cattle broker, he might be booted out. Or forced to eat tofu. That was the reason Logan had used cash when he checked in. No sense risking someone recognizing his name from his credit card.

The clerk had seemed to doubt him when Logan had told him that his ID and credit cards had been stolen and that was why he couldn't produce anything with his name on it. Of course, when Logan had slipped the guy an extra hundred-dollar bill, it had caused that doubt to disappear.

"Drinking your troubles away?" a woman asked.

"Trying."

Though he wasn't drunk enough that he couldn't see what was waiting for him at the end of this. A hangover, a missed 8:00 a.m. meeting, his family worried about him—the puking—and it wouldn't fix anything other than to give him a couple hours of mind-numbing solace.

At the moment though, mind-numbing solace, even if it was temporary, seemed like a good trade-off.

"Me, too," she said. "Drinking my troubles away."

Judging from the sultry tone in her voice, Logan first thought she might be a prostitute, but then he got a look at her.

Nope. Not a pro.

Or if she was, she'd done nothing to market herself as such. No low-cut dress to show her cleavage. She had on a T-shirt with cartoon turtles on the front, a baggy white skirt and flip-flops. It looked as if she'd grabbed the first items of clothing she could find off a very cluttered floor of her very cluttered apartment.

Logan wasn't into clutter.

And he'd thought Helene wasn't, either. He'd been wrong about that, too. That antique desk of hers had been plenty cluttered with a clown's bare ass.

"Mind if I join you?" Miss Turtle-Shirt said. "I'm having sort of a private going-away party."

She waited until Logan mumbled "suit yourself," and she slid onto the purple bar stool next to him.

She smelled like limes.

Her hair was varying shades of pink and looked as if it'd been cut with a weed whacker. It was already messy, but apparently it wasn't messy enough for her because she dragged her hand through it, pushing it away from her face.

"Tequila, top-shelf. Four shots and a bowl of lime slices," she told the bartender.

Apparently, he wasn't the only person in San Antonio with plans to get drunk tonight. And it explained the lime scent. These clearly weren't her first shots of the night.

"Do me a favor though," she said to Logan after he downed his next drink. "Don't ask my name, or anything personal about me, and I'll do the same for you."

Logan had probably never agreed to anything so fast in all his life. For one thing, he really didn't want to spend time talking with this woman, and he especially didn't want to talk about what'd happened.

"If you feel the need to call me something, go with Julia," she added.

The name definitely wasn't a fit. He was expecting something more like Apple or Sunshine. Still, he didn't care what she called herself. Didn't care what her real name was, either, and he cared even less after his next shot of Glenlivet.

"So, you're a cowboy, huh?" she asked.

The mind-numbing hadn't kicked in yet, but the orneriness had. "That's personal."

She shrugged. "Not really. You're wearing a cowboy hat, cowboy boots and jeans. It was more of an observation than a question."

"The clothes could be fashion statements," he pointed out.

Julia shook her head, downed the first shot of tequila, sucked on a lime slice. Made a face and shuddered. "You're not the kind of man to make fashion statements."

If he hadn't had a little buzz going on, he might have been insulted by that. "Unlike you?"

She glanced down at her clothes as if seeing them for the first time. Or maybe she was just trying to focus because the tequila had already gone to her head. "This was the first thing I grabbed off my floor."

Bingo. If that was her first grab, there was no telling how bad things were beneath it.

Julia tossed back her second shot. "Have you ever found out something that changed your whole life?" she asked.

"Yeah." About four hours ago.

"Me, too. Without giving specifics, because that would be personal, did it make you feel as if fate were taking a leak on your head?"

"Five leaks," he grumbled. Logan finished off his next shot.

Julia made a sound of agreement. "I would compare yours with mine, and I'd win, but I don't want to go there. Instead, let's play a drinking game."

"Let's not," he argued. "And in a fate-pissing comparison, I don't think you'd win."

Julia made a sound of disagreement. Had another shot. Grimaced and shuddered again. "So, the game is a word association," she continued as if he'd agreed. "I say a word, you say the first thing that comes to mind. We take turns until we're too drunk to understand what the other one is saying."

Until she'd added that last part, Logan had been about to get up and move to a different spot. But hell, he was getting drunk anyway, and at least this way he'd have some company. Company he'd never see again. Company he might not even be able to speak to if the slurring went up a notch.

"Dream?" she threw out there.

"Family." That earned him a sound of approval from her, and she motioned for him to take his turn. "Surprise?"

"Crappy," Julia said without hesitation.

Now it was Logan who made a grunt of approval. Surprises could indeed be crap-related. The one he'd gotten tonight certainly had been.

Her: "Tattoos?"

Him: "None." Then, "You?"

Her: "Two." Then, "Bucket list?"

Him: "That's two words." The orneriness was still there despite the buzz.

Her: "Just bucket, then?"

Too late. Logan's fuzzy mind was already fixed on the bucket list. He had one all right. Or rather he'd had one. A life with Helene that included all the trimmings, and this stupid game was a reminder that the Glenlivet wasn't working nearly fast enough. So, he had another shot.

Julia had one as well. "Sex?" she said.

Logan shook his head. "I don't want to play this game anymore."

When she didn't respond, Logan looked at her. Their eyes met. Eyes that were already slightly unfocused.

Julia took the paper sleeve with her room key from her pocket. Except there were two keys, and she slid one Logan's way.

"It's not the game," she explained. "I'm offering you sex with me. No names. No strings attached. Just one night, and we'll never tell another soul about it."

She finished off her last tequila shot, shuddered and stood. "Are you game?"

No way, and Logan would have probably said that to her if she hadn't leaned in and kissed him.

Maybe it was the weird combination of her tequila and his scotch, or maybe it was because he was already drunker than he thought, but Logan felt himself moving right into that kiss.

LOGAN DREAMED, AND it wasn't about the great sex he'd just had. It was another dream that wasn't so pleasant. The night of his parents' car accident. Some dreams were a mishmash of reality and stuff that didn't make sense. But this dream always got it right.

Not a good thing.

It was like being trapped on a well-oiled hamster wheel, seeing the same thing come up over and over again and not being able to do a thing to stop it.

The dream rain felt and sounded so real. Just like that night. It was coming down so hard that the moment his truck wipers swished it away, the drops covered the windshield again. That was why it'd taken him so long to see the lights, and Logan was practically right on the scene of the wreck before he could fully brake. He went into a skid, costing him precious seconds. If he'd had those seconds, he could have called the ambulance sooner.

He could have saved them.

But he hadn't then. And he didn't now in the dream.

Logan chased away the images, and with his head still groggy, he did what he always did after the nightmare. He rewrote it. He got to his parents and stopped them from dying.

Every time except when it really mattered, Logan saved them.

LOGAN WISHED HE could shoot out the sun. It was creating lines of light on each side of the curtains, and those lines were somehow managing to stab through his closed eyelids. That was probably because every nerve in his head and especially his eyelids were screaming at him, and anything—including the earth's rotation—added to his pain.

He wanted to ask himself: *What the hell have you done?*

But he knew. He'd had sex with a woman he didn't know. A woman who wore turtle T-shirts and had tattoos. He'd learned one of the tattoos, a rose, was on Julia's right breast. The other was on her lower stomach. Those were the things Logan could actually remember.

That, and the sex.

Not mind-numbing but rather more mind-blowing. Julia clearly didn't have any trouble being wild and spontaneous in bed. It was as if she'd just studied a sex manual and wanted to try every position. Thankfully, despite the scotch, Logan had been able to keep up—literally.

Not so much now though.

If the fire alarm had gone off and the flames had been burning his ass, he wasn't sure he would be able to move. Julia didn't have that problem though. He felt the mattress shift when she got up. Since it was possible she was about to rob him, Logan figured he should at least see if she was going after his wallet, wherever the heck it was. But if she robbed him, he deserved it. His life was on the fast track to hell, and he'd been the one to put it in the handbasket.

At least he hadn't been so drunk that he'd forgotten to use condoms. Condoms that Julia had provided, so obviously she'd been ready for this sort of thing.

Logan heard some more stirring around, and this time the movement was very close to him. Just in case Julia turned out to be a serial killer, he decided to risk opening one eye. And he nearly jolted at the big green eyeball staring back at him. Except it wasn't a human eye. It was on her turtle shirt.

If Julia felt the jolt or saw his one eye opening, she didn't say anything about it. She gave him a chaste kiss on the cheek, moved away, turning her back to him, and Logan watched as she stooped down and picked up his jacket. So, not a serial killer but rather just a thief after all. But she didn't take anything out.

She put something *in* the pocket.

Logan couldn't tell what it was exactly. Maybe her number. Which he would toss first chance he got. But if so, he couldn't figure out why she just hadn't left it on the bed.

Julia picked up her purse, hooking it over her shoulder, and without even glancing back at him, she walked out the door. Strange, since this was her room. Maybe she was headed out to get them some coffee. If so, that was his cue to dress and get the devil out of there before she came back.

Easier said than done.

His hair hurt.

He could feel every strand of it on his head. His eyelashes, too. Still, Logan forced himself from the bed, only to realize the soles of his feet hurt as well. It was hard to identify something on him that didn't hurt, so he quit naming parts and put on his boxers and jeans. Then he had a look at what Julia had put in his pocket next to the box with the engagement ring.

A gold watch.

Not a modern one. It was old with a snap-up top

that had a crest design on it. The initials BWS had been engraved in the center of the crest.

The inside looked just as expensive as the gold case except for the fact that the watch face crystal inside was shattered. Even though he knew little about antiques, Logan figured it was worth at least a couple hundred dollars.

So, why had Julia put it in his pocket?

Since he was a skeptic, his first thought was that she might be trying to set him up, to make it look as if he'd robbed her. But Logan couldn't imagine why anyone would do that unless she was planning to try to blackmail him with it.

He dropped the watch on the bed and finished dressing, all the while staring at it. He cleared out some of the cotton in his brain and grabbed the hotel phone to call the front desk. Someone answered on the first ring.

"I'm in room—" Logan had to check the phone "—two-sixteen, and I need to know..." He had to stop again and think. "I need to know if Julia is there in the lobby. She left something in the room."

"No, sir. I'm afraid you just missed her. But checkout isn't until noon, and she said her guest might be staying past then, so she paid for an extra day."

"Uh, could you tell me how to spell Julia's last name? I need to leave her a note in case she comes back."

"Oh, she said she wouldn't be coming back, that this was her goodbye party. And as for how to spell her name, well, it's Child, just like it sounds."

Julia Child?

Right. Obviously, the clerk wasn't old enough or enough of a foodie to recognize the name of the famous chef.

"I don't suppose she paid with a credit card?" Logan asked.

"No. She paid in cash and then left a prepaid credit card for the second night."

Of course. "What about an address?" Logan kept trying.

"I'm really not supposed to give that out—"

"She left something very expensive in the room, and I know she'll want it back."

The guy hemmed and hawed a little, but he finally rattled off, "221B Baker Street, London, England."

That was Sherlock Holmes's address.

Logan groaned, cursed. He didn't bother asking for a phone number because the one she left was probably for Hogwarts. He hung up and hurried to the window, hoping he could get a glimpse of her getting into a car. Not that he intended to follow her or anything, but if she was going to blackmail him, he wanted to know as much about her as possible.

No sign of her, but Logan got a flash of something else. A memory.

Damn.

They'd taken pictures.

Or at least Julia had with the camera on her phone. He remembered nude selfies of them from the waist up. At least he hoped it was from the waist up.

Yeah, that trip to hell in a handbasket was moving even faster right now.

Logan threw on the rest of his clothes, already trying to figure out how to do damage control. He was the CEO of a multimillion-dollar company. He was the face that people put with the family business, and before last night he'd never done a thing to tarnish the image of McCord Cattle Brokers.

He couldn't say that any longer.

He was in such a hurry to rush out the door that he nearly missed the note on the desk. Maybe it was the start of the blackmail. He snatched it up, steeling himself up for the worst. But if this was blackmail, then Julia sure had a funny sense of humor.

"Goodbye, hot cowboy," she'd written. "Thanks for the sweet send-off. Don't worry. What happens in San Antonio stays in San Antonio. I'll take this to the grave."

Don't miss
BLAME IT ON THE COWBOY
by Delores Fossen,
available October 2016 wherever
HQN Books and ebooks are sold.

www.Harlequin.com

Dr. Michelson pulled back the blue curtain. "Where's
Tessa and the baby?"

Landon practically pushed the doctor aside and looked
into the room. No Tessa. No baby. But the door leading
off the back of the examining room was open.

"Close off all the exits," Landon told the doctor, and
he took off after her.

He cursed Tessa, and himself, for this. He should have
known she would run, and when he caught up with her,
she'd better be able to explain why she'd done this.

Landon barreled through the adjoining room. Another
exam room, crammed with equipment that he had to
maneuver around. He also checked the corners in case
she had ducked behind something with plans to sneak out
after he'd zipped right past her.

But she wasn't there, either.

There was a hall just off the examining room, and Landon headed there, his gaze slashing from one end of it to the other. He didn't see her.

But he heard something.

The baby.

She was still crying, and even though the sound was muffled, it was enough for Landon to pinpoint their location. Tessa was headed for the back exit. Landon doubted the doctor had managed to get the doors locked yet, so he hurried, running as fast as he could.

And then he saw her.

Tessa saw him, too.

She didn't stop. With the baby gripped in her arms, she threw open the glass door and was within a heartbeat of reaching the parking lot. She might have made it, too, but Landon took hold of her arms and pulled her back inside.

As he'd done by the barn, he was as gentle with her as he could be, but he wasn't feeling very much of that gentleness inside.

Tessa was breathing through her mouth. Her eyes were wide. And she groaned. "I remember," she said.

He jerked back his head. That was the last thing Landon had expected her to say, but he'd take it. "Yeah, and you're going to tell me everything you remember, and you're going to do it right now."

JUST CAN'T GET ENOUGH?

Join our social communities
and talk to us online.

You will have access to the latest
news on upcoming titles and special
promotions, but most importantly,
you can talk to other fans about your
favorite Harlequin reads.

Harlequin.com/Community

Facebook.com/HarlequinBooks

Twitter.com/HarlequinBooks

Pinterest.com/HarlequinBooks

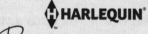